THE BOSS OF EVERYONE!

DANNY WALLACE

Illustrated by gemma CORRELL

SIMON & SCHUSTER

First published in Great Britain in 2023 by Simon & Schuster UK Ltd

1 3 5 7 9 10 8 6 4 2

Simon & Schuster UK Ltd
1st Floor, 222 Gray's Inn Road, London
WC1X 8HB

www.simonandschuster.co.uk
www.simonandschuster.com.au
www.simonandschuster.co.in

Simon & Schuster Australia, Sydney
Simon & Schuster India, New Delhi

A CIP catalogue record for this book is available from the British Library.

PB ISBN 978-1-3985-1738-7
eBook ISBN 978-1-3985-1739-4
eAudio ISBN 978-1-3985-1740-0

Typeset in the UK
Printed and Bound in the UK using 100% Renewable Electricity
at CPI Group (UK) Ltd

MIX
Paper from
responsible sources
FSC® C171272

THE BOSS OF EVERYONE!

Also by Danny Wallace

The Day the Screens Went Blank

The Luckiest Kid in the World

Hamish and the WorldStoppers

Hamish and the Neverpeople

Hamish and the GravityBurp

Hamish and the Baby BOOM!

Hamish and the Monster Patrol

Hamish and the Terrible Terrible
Christmas and other Stories

For my mum,
who taught me how to see
the good in everyone,
and who's shown her grandchildren
the very same.

CHAPTER ONE

Are you sitting up straight?

No? Well . . .

Are you sitting up straight . . . *now?!*

One, two, three – eyes on me!

It's your own time you're wasting. I can do this all day!

Well, actually, I can't, so let's just start the lesson.

I mean, the STORY!

Because this is the story of how one girl (me) got the best job in the world ever.

So how did I do it? How did I become *my dad's actual boss?*

Let's start in the most magical, wonderful place on Earth. Let's start in a place where dreams come true, where the sun always shines, where the smells of clean hallways and freshly scrubbed toilets dance across your nose like pure fairy dust.

SCHOOL!

Just like you, I absolutely love school. Can't get enough of the place.

At school, every day is a lesson. In fact, every *lesson* is a lesson.

My name is Joss Pilfrey

and I'm in my last year at Twin Pines Primary. Next year I'll go to Woodhall Secondary School, which I cannot wait for. I've already memorized where all the buildings are so that I don't waste any time getting lost when I could be learning. My new school will be the making of me. All my current teachers are very keen for me to go.

For now, I'm doing my best to get as much out of the time I have left at Twin Pines as possible.

I have been made Star of the Week more times than anyone else. You get made Star of the Week if you get the most gold stars on the Star Chart for star-like behaviour.

I am the person who makes sure all the art stuff is put away properly, so I get a star for that.

I'm always first to get into my gym kit and I'm always last out of the classroom, once I've made sure all the windows have been shut properly and the guinea pig has water. A classroom pet is not supposed to be fun – as I always remind everybody – it is merely a way of developing responsibility.

And when a question is asked, or a volunteer is needed, I always, ALWAYS put my hand up.

I also study the teachers very carefully to make sure they are doing everything correctly, and I am quick to point out when they've stuffed up. I provide this service absolutely free of charge – although I don't seem to get many stars for that.

Yes, I feel I am ready to progress to the next level in school and life, which is what I tell my head teacher every lunchtime when I eat my sandwiches in her office and tell her what the other teachers have done wrong.

'Wouldn't you rather go and play with all the other kids?' she asks. But no, I have done this every single day since I started at Twin Pines. It's a good chance for me to learn what makes my head teacher tick. I am sure she appreciates it. She deserves to have someone paying such great attention to everything she does, because she really does work so hard.

Really she does.

'You can't come in,' she might say when I knock, 'because I've got a lot of work to do.'

Or: 'Please don't come to the office this lunchtime, Joss,' she'll go, 'as I really do have a lot of work to be getting on with!'

If I walk in and she's not at her desk, I check her cupboard, because sometimes she's working on her phone in there, even if I've told her I'm coming!

Sometimes she's got to do playground duty, which is even better. Then I stand alongside her, making sure no one's getting up to any mischief.

'Join in, Joss!' she'll say, but I know she could do with the extra pair of eyes. I like to think of myself as her shadow. I only do this to be helpful and because I've got so many important questions for her.

'Why do you do things this way? Why do you do things that way? Wouldn't it be better if you did it like the other schools do it?'

But as she points out, I don't need to sit in her office or follow her about all day, because I've got plenty of chances to ask her all this stuff at home. Because Mrs Pilfrey isn't just my head teacher – she's also my mum.

CHAPTER TWO

A lot of kids get embarrassed if they put their hand up in school and accidentally call the teacher 'Mum'. I do too, but only because it makes me look unprofessional. We're all working towards what we want to be when we grow up. I want to be somebody important like Mum, but my job now is to be a pupil, and it is one I take seriously.

Even at our house, when it is just me and my parents, I always remember I am representing my school. I try to keep my uniform on for as long as possible and then I sleep in pyjamas in school colours (purple and yellow, a lovely combination).

My mum tries to get me to relax. 'You're ten,' she'll say, looking exasperated. 'Have some fun!'

But I'll tell her I had plenty of time for fun when I was a baby. And what exactly did that achieve?

She's always trying to get to me to join afterschool clubs or hang out with other kids, but I would rather stay at home. The other kids actually want to go to the park and run around but I am not a natural athlete. I am more an athlete of the mind. An Olympian of organization!

Once a week, Mrs Pilfrey (aka Mum) goes out

with some of the other teachers to 'unwind' and due to the law, I am left with Bob (aka Dad).

Bob is very normal for an adult, but he knows very little about how children work. He works for a company where they make outdoor toys. Hula hoops, skipping ropes, stomp rockets, that sort of thing. I remember when I was little, he would bring things like this home for me. He stopped when he realized I was more into having my own personalised marker pens, but I do remember being happy when he brought back a Swingball. I don't know where that is any more. Anyway, I should probably try and show more interest in his work. It would be very encouraging for Bob.

Mum wishes I'd stop calling her 'Mrs Pilfrey' at home and start calling her 'Mum', and Bob thinks me calling him 'Bob' is weird and asks why I can't call him 'Dad'.

But as I've told Bob a million times, I call Mum 'Mrs Pilfrey' out of respect, and it would be *dis*respectful to her if I showed *him* the same respect. He is less of a 'senior' figure in the household, I tell him. It's not his fault, but Dad's not quite like Mum. She is a leader, like me. Dad is what you'd call a worker bee. A pencil pusher. He is very competent, but he has not excelled in the way my mum has. But he does his best, and he makes great hot chocolate. I don't know what his secret is. Maybe I should ask him more questions.

I know the 'Mrs Pilfrey' and 'Bob' thing is probably confusing though so I'll just call them Mum and Dad in this to make things easier for you.

Dad leaves for work after we do in the mornings. The company he works for is called Griffin Games. I'm not one hundred per cent sure what he does there but I know he's got his own desk.

At the door, he kisses Mum on the cheek and wishes her luck with the journey (I always wonder why – it's just a five-minute drive and a great chance for me to quiz her on what she hopes to achieve for the day), and I shake his hand because otherwise he will ruffle my hair and mess up my ponytail.

We leave for school one hour earlier than everyone else so that we can be first to arrive. Dad says he'd be more than happy to take me in later so that I arrive at the same time as all the other kids.

'You can join in with whatever they're doing!' he says, but that would mean I wouldn't get to sit in the staffroom, making sure all the other teachers have completed their lesson plans for the day. Mum says to stop doing that, but I don't think she can be serious.

The other kids in class think I do all this because I have never been made Class Monitor. It is the job I was born to do. If I were Class Monitor, everyone would have to listen to me, and I would try to have ideas that helped

everyone get the best out of themselves. In our class, it is Mohammed who has that job right now. He is very popular and always makes jokes when he does the register. I have to keep reminding him that doing the register is a great honour and he should treat it as such. You would think they would let me do it when Mohammed is away, but Mrs Bonney always lets Sarah do it instead – just because 'she is very shy and this is a great way to boost her confidence!'.

I sit next to Sarah and try to help her with her confidence because maybe then she won't have to do the register. She is quite like a fragile little mouse, which can be frustrating. She needs some get-up-and-go. The way I help her with

SARAH

13

her confidence is to point out what she could do better. Again, totally free of charge.

I notice Mrs Bonney always spends a little extra time with Sarah, saying encouraging things, and I feel bad because it makes me a bit jealous. Sarah is not a great chatterbox but that's okay because I always have a lot to say, so I take care of that (when appropriate of course).

I suppose Sarah is the closest I have to a friend, but you would have to ask her. I'm not sure what she'd say. I don't think I have that many 'proper' friends, but that's okay. Mum sometimes tries to arrange hangouts with different kids for me, but they usually start cancelling after one or two playdates. I think some kids don't like it that as soon as they get to my house I give them one of two options: a head start on our homework or watching something educational online.

I think if you could call me and Sarah 'friends', it is a friendship based on mutual respect and a quiet work ethic.

Our classroom is great. Mrs Bonney is always asking questions or calling out for volunteers. Dad says it's important to 'grab every opportunity' so I always put my hand up. If Sarah ever puts her hand up, it is miles after I do it, like she doesn't really want to answer. So, I strain and block her from view slightly, ensuring that I get to answer, which is my way of inspiring her further.

There are lots of encouraging posters on the classroom wall and

STAR CHART

Sarah ★ ★ ★
Jack ★ ★
Amir ★ ★ ★ ★
Evie ★ ★
Kwame ★ ★ ★
Joss ★ ★ ★ ★ ★ ★ ★
Mohammed ★ ★

we put our best art up. There's also our Star Chart (I am ahead on Positivity, Participation *and* Politeness already this week!). When someone does something outstanding, Mrs Bonney rings her WELL BELL and shouts, 'You're doing WELL!'

To help her encourage us, I come up with new and motivational slogans to pin up above the whiteboard at the start of each day. It's one of the things I learned from my at-home research on good school techniques. I write things like 'Work HARDER!' or 'Be SILENT!'.

Mrs Bonney takes them down every night without fail, which I think is her way of encouraging me to do new ones every morning to replace them.

Like me, Sarah doesn't really do much playing at break. We are supposed to get fresh air and eat fruit because it helps us concentrate. I am yet to see the science on this, but I am willing to go along with it for now.

I see Sarah sitting on her own a lot at breaktime. Or she'll stand at the edge of the playground, watching the other kids jump around. She is definitely a bit of a loner. She wears a big blue duffle coat like Paddington Bear and red gloves and looks over at me sometimes. We both have brown hair and ponytails and we both wear Dr. Martens boots on the weekends. I want to go and talk to her, but I am usually busy because I also have to keep my eye on kids like Jack Davis.

Jack's bigger than the other kids. Well, actually, he isn't. He's the same size. He just acts bigger. He's the kind of kid who will take your

ball off you and go and play with it somewhere else. He eats apples in a really angry way. No one stands up to him because he thinks he can do what he wants. Even when I point that out to a teacher, they just sort of let it happen. If I was Class Monitor, I would use that power to stop him. I suppose that's the one thing that annoys me. I don't have any power. If I had power, I could use it to make things better for everybody. I could introduce a simple ball-sharing system or hand out detentions to kids like Jack. But at the end of the day, no matter what I do, I'm just a ten-year-old kid.

Still. All that's about to change.

CHAPTER THREE

'Children!' says Mrs Bonney, right after Friday register.

I immediately put my hand up in case this is a question or a call for volunteers, but she shakes her head at me, so I put it down again.

'Children!' she says again, trying to settle everyone down. 'One, two, three – eyes on me!'

Everyone stops chatting. I am so impressed

by this trick and always have been. It's like pure magic. It's like a teacher miracle. I raise my eyebrows at Sarah to show I am impressed and that perhaps she should be too.

'I have some very interesting news,' continues Mrs Bonney.

Well, it *must* be very interesting. Because our wise and generous leader Mum has popped into the classroom herself to witness it! I nudge Sarah to get her to sit up straighter.

Mrs Bonney is holding up a letter from the local council. Perhaps the mayor got my email petition and I'm about to be made Class Monitor! I feel a shiver of excitement. I look up at Mum and she looks back, pleased as punch.

'Monday next week will be a very special Monday,' Mrs Bonney says, and Mum gives me two thumbs up, like I'm really going to love this. 'Your parents or carers should all have had their letters this morning, because on Monday it's Take Your Kid to Work Day!'

There is a gasp in the room. I am shocked. Mum did not warn me about this at all!

'So, we don't have to come to school?' asks Jack Davis, which is typical, and then everyone applauds.

Polly says she's going to work as her mum's assistant lifeguard at the leisure centre.

Vijay says he'll be at the bookshop in town with his stepdad and claps his hands together.

Jack says he'll be temporary head chef at the family café, making the sandwiches! (I expect I'll be reading a lot of 'food poisoning' stories in the local paper soon.)

And I notice I am applauding now – because for me, too, Take Your Kid to Work Day is the very best news possible.

'It doesn't mean not coming to school for me,'

I tell Sarah. 'It means *more* school!'

No wonder Mum was so excited for me. I won't have to do any lessons. I'll be able to hang out with her, the *whole day*. I'll be able to ask her question after question – morning, noon and night. I'll be able to go to meetings, make suggestions and eat biscuits in the staffroom with her and all the other teachers all day long! It's just so annoying that there's a whole weekend to get through first.

'Each of you will get the chance to see what a real workplace is like,' says Mrs Bonney. 'And the exciting things grown-ups get up to!'

I cannot wait for Monday! I'm so excited I forget Mum is my head teacher and I put my hand up and say, 'Mum! We're going to have such fun!'

'You certainly are!' she says. 'You're going to learn about so many different things!'

Hoorah!

'A chance for some real parent time,' she says.

Yahoo!

'And I know your dad is really looking forward to having you there!'

Hang on. What?

When we get home, it seems like Dad didn't really know this was going to happen either.

'I must have forgotten to tell you, Bob,' says Mum at dinner, looking shifty and trying to avoid his eye. 'All the primary schools in town are doing it for Joss's year group. But it'll be fine! A chance to show Joss what *you* do, too. And everyone at school agrees it would be *really* good for all of the children.'

Dad nods to himself, then says, 'But wouldn't

you like more Joss time?'

'I have . . . a lot of Joss time.' She smiles sweetly. '*So* much Joss time.'

'But Monday's the day of the big meeting,' says Dad. 'Pop Griffin himself is coming in! Am I just supposed to take Joss to the meeting? What if it lasts all day?'

Personally, I've always wanted to go to a big business meeting. Maybe one at a bank where I can shout and then fire someone. But I still don't know why it's not Mum taking me to her work. We could have a big business meeting there. I have loads of ideas for very long staff meetings.

'It will be good for Joss to see there's a world *outside* school. And it'll be good for people like Pop Griffin and Mr Jackson to see you as an actual person, with a family, Bob,' says Mum. 'Not just someone with a desk.'

'I don't know,' says Dad. 'It's very late notice. And the meeting! It's . . . important!'

They're talking like I'm not here. I need to make my opinion known. I put my arm up straight and wave my hand around.

'Joss, for the hundredth time, you don't have to put your hand up at home,' says Dad. 'Yes, you can go to the toilet.'

'No, it's not that,' I say. 'It's more . . . well, don't take this the wrong way, Bob. But I don't really know anything about what you do. I don't really know about your work, or who you work with, or really what it is you *do* at Griffin Games. I've never even been to your office.'

Dad nods, almost a little sadly. 'So, what are you saying, Joss?'

'I guess what I'm saying,' I tell him, 'is . . . wouldn't it be better if I went with *Mum* to *her* work?'

Mum gives Dad a Look.

Dad sighs, then sits up, his expression determined.

'Right,' he says. 'You're coming with me on Monday. The world of outdoor toy sales awaits you! An opportunity to be grabbed! You should know what I do. It'll be . . . a bonding experience.'

Well, that backfired spectacularly.

CHAPTER FOUR

I kept busy all weekend with my scheduled reading and drawing time, and also by working on a new colour-coded timetable for school and ideas for extra homework. It is important to stay distracted when you have things you don't want to think about.

It's not that I don't want to go to Dad's work. It's more that I'm worried about how school will function without me.

School is all about routine, and if I am not there to help enforce that, what will all the teachers do? If anything, this is unfair on them. They may well fall to pieces without me.

Instead, I'm being sent to Dad's work, where I won't know how to be useful.

'You don't need to be useful!' Dad reassures me that night, as I get into my casual weekend pyjamas rather than my formal weeknight ones. 'It's okay to just be a kid!'

Nevertheless, I will do my best to make a great impression as a representative of the Pilfrey family. I like to make people proud. And I want to be useful.

SAND TIMER

If Mrs Bonney sets us a task, she will sometimes use a sand timer, so that we can all see how long we have left to

EYEBROWS

concentrate. And if the class gets rowdy and loud, she won't shout. She'll just stand at the front of the class with her eyebrows raised until we realize what she's doing and settle down. Nobody wants to get computer time taken away or to miss break. She's also very generous with the Star Chart. I do really like getting gold star stickers for good work or for being helpful. I have learned a lot of useful techniques and handy tactics like these from my teachers over the years. If I had any brothers or sisters, I would definitely use the eyebrow technique on them.

STICKERS

Well done!

I just get the feeling that when I go to Dad's work, I won't get any stickers at all and I won't have Mrs Bonney there to help everyone concentrate. You very rarely see grown-ups with stickers, and this is one of the great tragedies of ageing.

But I have to look on the bright side: tomorrow, I will be able to sit in a very long business meeting for AGES.

'Have a great day together! Enjoy yourself, Joss!' yells Mum, as she leaves for work. She whips the front door shut behind her so quickly the doorknocker bangs twice. All the teachers are going to do an away day together instead of their usual lovely staffroom meetings, poor things. It's at a local spa, so I imagine they will be doing lesson plans on Roman water sources. They don't even get a proper lunch, Mum said. They have to do something called a 'Bottomless Brunch'!

I hope that doesn't mean they're not allowed to wear trousers.

I *am* wearing trousers. Smart ones. And my smartest black top. I have arranged my hair into my usual smart ponytail, and I have brought my own clipboard because it makes me look smart and ready for action. I said 'smart' a lot there.

SMART
PONYTAIL

SMART
TOP

CLIPBOARD
(MAKES
ME LOOK
SMART)

SMART
TROUSERS

SMART
SHOES

Dad and I sit in the kitchen in silence. It is interesting to see what he does with this extra hour he has. It is like being in Dad World. What he mainly does is drink coffee and eat toast while the clock on the wall ticks loudly.

Is this really what grown-ups do when we're not around?

I feel like we need a pre-work meeting.

'So, what are your expectations for the day ahead?' I ask, and Dad nearly chokes on his toast.

'My expectations?' he says. 'Er, look. Just come in. Meet everybody. Don't set anything on fire. And then we'll come home.'

I frown.

'It would just be handy to know my role in the company,' I say. 'So, I can be useful.'

'Your role? Well, once again, your role is to be a kid, just like other people's kids will be doing. I'll show you where I sit. You can see the

32

kitchenette. You can spin on my chair!'

Spin on his chair? I don't think Dad is taking this very seriously at all.

Dad must love his job because he goes there every day, even though he is always clicking through the websites looking for a new one.

The only problem he has with his job is that he was definitely sure he was going to get a promotion last year but then for some reason he didn't. I remember him saying he had been at Griffin Games ages and was always doing loads of extra work. But then they had given the job to a man called Mr Jackson instead, and he'd only just joined the company. Dad said it wasn't fair.

I totally get how Dad feels about that. It's just like my Class Monitor thing.

Griffin Games is over on the other side of town in a tall building next to a car park.

On the drive there, Dad tells me that he usually joins a big queue of workmates to grab a breakfast steak bake and a second coffee from the place opposite, even though he's already had breakfast at home!

The building is called Griffin Tower and even though it's home to Griffin Games, it doesn't say that anywhere. Dad parks the car, and

amazingly, I go from slightly grumpy to slightly excited. It's not as cool as school, but it is a very grown-up place. Everyone is walking straight in through the door with their bags and their steak bakes. I notice a distinct lack of clipboards but maybe they are just hidden in their work bags. They're all staring at the ground as they walk, looking very serious, probably determined to get a great day's work done. No one is hanging about outside in the drizzle, waiting for their friends. No one is running around, being silly or laughing. I haven't seen a single person try to push someone else into a bush. I have to say, I am impressed. Maybe I can take this discipline back and apply it to Twin Pines Primary.

'I wonder how many other kids will be here,' I say as we get to the door, because suddenly my excitement turns to nerves. Something about the idea of a whole building of new people reminds me that soon I'll be going to Woodhall Secondary. I mean, that's exciting, and of course it will be the making of me, but I sometimes feel nervous when I remember.

'I'm not sure,' says Dad, and then he puts his hand on my shoulder and looks at me, all serious. 'I know you'll behave, J, because I can't remember the last time you misbehaved. But still – when we go inside – we're in my grown-up world. So: behave.'

I am shocked that he feels the need to tell me this. When Mum and Dad have friends round, and all I can hear from downstairs is mad laughter and bottles being clanked near the kitchen bin, it is me who has to come down and tell them the fun's over and it's bedtime. It usually works. My record is half past nine. But I think Dad is just saying it because he thinks it's a dad thing to do.

So in we go!

My first impression of my dad's desk is that it is very messy. He hasn't put any of his pens away. There are little scraps of paper everywhere. This is very disappointing.

DAD'S DESK ↓

There are about seven or eight people in the office, all at their own messy desks, and a few of them have already looked over at me in a very quizzical manner. Apparently Dad's the only one who's brought his kid to work.

Dad decides the best thing to do is show me round with great enthusiasm.

'Angela! Let me introduce you to my daughter, Joss, who I have brought here today because it's Take Your Kid to Work Day!'

He says this loudly, so everyone can hear why he has brought a child in.

'Hello, Joss,' says Angela, like she has no idea what to say to a kid.

'Good morning to you,' I say, in a very business-like manner.

Dad turns to a man who's still munching on a steak bake. This might seem unfair to comment on, but his shirt is half untucked and a bit stained, and someone should really tell him about combs.

'Barry, did you not bring your kids in?' asks Dad.

'I thought it best not to,' replies Barry. 'Because

of the meeting. And also, I forgot.'

Dad nods, then turns to a woman in the corner.

'What about you, Fiona?'

Fiona seems embarrassed.

'Well, we've got the meeting . . .' she says. 'And you know what Mr Jackson is like.'

On the way in, Dad had given me a little run-down of all the people who work at Griffin Games.

There was Mr Jackson, of course, who he said was 'an acquired taste' which is grown-up speak for not very nice. He says Mr Jackson thinks he knows best but that is not always the case. He also made me promise not to tell anyone that, so I'd appreciate it if you kept it to yourself.

Then there was Angela, a 'dog person' and a great worker who quite liked to keep herself to herself.

There was untidy Barry who never met a shirt he couldn't spill food down.

There was Tim and Kareem who have lots of ideas but never seem to tell anyone about them and also don't really get on with each other. They squabble a lot.

Fiona was good at her job but a bit scared of Mr Jackson and went along with anything he said.

And there was Sleepy Ken, who . . . well, he said I'd work out Sleepy Ken on my own.

I always imagined that Dad's office would be full of Griffin Games games. I thought there'd be a big green bouncy castle in the corner, and maybe some of their other outdoor toys, like glittery hula hoops or slides or a giant wooden bricks game. But Dad says all that stuff is downstairs, packed up in boxes in the basement. Up here, it's basically a grey room full of grey desks. There is a clock on the wall and that seems to be the only entertainment. Apart from the clock, it looks like the most fun you can have is either sitting on a spinning chair or turning on the kettle. Of course, this is a good thing. People are here to work, not be entertained by kettles.

There are a few signs on a corkboard. They're mainly things like PLEASE REMEMBER TO WASH UP YOUR OWN MUG or DO NOT STEAL OTHER PEOPLE'S SNACKS. I approve of these signs. They are very direct and effective.

And there are also some useful ones, like REMEMBER TO USE THE DOORSTOP IN THE STOCKROOM OTHERWISE YOU WILL END UP LOCKED IN THERE FOR EVER.

I am suddenly terrified of the stockroom.

Just then, the guy who got Dad's job – Mr Jackson – comes in and immediately spots me. He puts his hands on his hips and sighs.

'Bob?' he asks, looking me up and down.

'No,' I say, pointing at Dad. *'That's* Bob.'

CHAPTER FIVE

Well, I don't really feel very welcome right now.

It turns out that Mr Jackson really expected everybody to *not* bring their kid to Take Your Kid to Work Day. He has fundamentally misunderstood the whole day!

From what I could hear him saying, there was '*a time and a place for fun and laughter – and it is NOT at Griffin Games!*'

Through the glass wall of his office, I hear Mr Jackson shouting words like 'unprofessional!' and 'important meeting!' and Dad keeps saying 'Take Your Kid to Work Day!' in a really pleading voice. I don't like the way Mr Jackson is acting towards my dad. I look round for someone to tell, but offices don't tend to have dinner ladies.

'Everyone knew this would happen,' whispers Angela to me. 'Mr Jackson wouldn't care if every school in the world was doing Take Your Kid to Work Day, he does not approve of things like this. Your poor dad.'

'You should have told him,' says Kareem to Tim.

Tim replies, 'Maybe *you* should have, Kareem!'

And then everybody round me gasps as the main office door flings open and a large older man enters. I immediately duck behind my clipboard.

As I peek round, I see the man is wearing a

POP
GRIFFIN

tartan waistcoat that is straining at the buttons. He has a cloud of white curly hair that makes his face seem red. He has a security access pass hanging round his neck and a big gold watch.

I know who this is. I've seen his picture. It's Pop Griffin himself.

Pop Griffin started Griffin Games in 1990, so he must be like two hundred years old. He began this whole company from the back of a van, and now sells his toys and games all over the world. He's also the guy who gave Mr Jackson the promotion instead of Dad. Apparently, he has been getting weirder and weirder over the years, and he always repeats himself, but Dad said we're never to mention that.

'Meeting room. Five minutes!' he growls, and everybody starts to gather their things together. 'Five minutes, meeting room!'

Finally, the moment I've been waiting for!

I must say, I feel a little uncomfortable being so smartly dressed when everyone round me is in their normal work clothes. Collars are bent, trousers too baggy. Hardly anyone is wearing a tie. I pop my clipboard on my lap and sit straight in my grown-up chair, ready to take notes. I am determined to be useful.

'So, here's what it is,' bellows Pop Griffin, addressing the room. 'What it is, is this. Griffin Games is headed downhill. Downhill, it's headed.

And I've had enough, I have. I've had enough.'

I decide it will be quicker if I just make a note of everything he says the first time.

'You lot have been taking the mickey, you have,' he says. 'You've lost your fire! Your energy! Your joy!'

Looking round at the grown-ups, all pale and slouchy, with steak bake stains down their rumpled tops, I can see his point. They do not look like what you'd call a crack team of office experts.

STEAK BAKE
STAIN

'You used to live for Griffin Games! But where has that enthusiasm gone? Down the toilet, along with our sales figures!'

You could almost hear the tummies drop. Everyone seemed like they were trying to hide under the table. It just made me sit up straighter. After all, none of this was *my* fault!

'I have to say I agree with you,' says Mr Jackson suddenly. 'The team really needs to pull together more. I tell them all the time. I don't know what's wrong with them. It's very hard to watch.'

Fiona looks totally shocked by Mr Jackson's rudeness.

'If I could just point out a few people who could improve,' he continues, but Pop Griffin cuts him off.

'I don't want to hear blame! Instead, I'm going to disappear on my boat for a week or so, switch my phone off, and decide what to do. I may sell the company. I may just shut it down. If you want to keep your jobs and keep Griffin Games going, it's up to you to show me a difference.'

There's a gasp in the room.

'As of now, until my return, I am no longer in charge of Griffin Games. So, who wants to be me?'

Nobody seemed to catch that last bit. So, for the first time, he repeated himself on purpose.

'I mean: who wants to be in charge? Give me an idea! A game-changer! A Griffin Games-changer!'

Wait. Was he saying . . . who wants to be in charge . . . of Griffin Games?!

'Technically, Mr Griffin, it should be me,' says Mr Jackson, standing up, all confident and more than a little bit smug.

'NOT you,' says Pop loudly. 'I want NEW ideas.'

Very subtly, I nudge Dad in the ribs. *Go for it,*

I'm thinking. *Grab your opportunity!*

'WELL?' asks Pop. 'Who's got an idea?'

'It's a test,' whispers Fiona. 'He's trying to see who wants to steal his job!'

I notice Tim widening his eyes, silently telling Kareem he should say something, and Kareem raising his eyebrows like *You say something if you're so good, Tim.*

I nudge Dad in the ribs again. He doesn't move. His hands stay down. This is his big chance! His big moment! Why won't he grab the opportunity? He could be Class Monitor!

'ANYONE?' says Pop. 'One little idea!'

He holds up the pass round his neck and shows it to us all. It says 'BOSS'.

'Who wants the BOSS pass?' he says. 'One of you can have the BOSS pass!'

I look up at Dad, pleadingly, but he stares straight ahead, frozen.

No one is answering. It is SO AWKWARD.

'An idea! An idea! A *volunteer*!' yells Pop, and that word, volunteer, has such an effect on me!

I can already feel it happening. It is the magic of the classroom. The call of contribution!

My fingers start to flutter on my knee.

Then my wrist rises.

Then my arm is off my leg.

'Last chance!' yells Pop.

And that's the final straw. I can't help it. My arm shoots straight up in the air and strains, like I'm trying to touch the ceiling.

'You!' yells Pop Griffin, pointing at me. 'What's your big idea?'

I clear my throat.

'Um . . . well, I heard that you can get locked in the stockroom if you forget to use the doorstop. Wouldn't it be better to fix that, so that people didn't get locked in the stockroom?'

A silence. Then . . .

Pop Griffin clears his throat.

Cracks a single knuckle.

Inhales deeply.

And says . . . 'THAT IS BRILLIANT THINKING!'

Oh! Good!

'What you're saying is very clever. What you're really saying is *"Only by fixing the small things can we fix the big things, by fixing the small things!"*'

Well, I didn't mean to, but okay.

'You're in charge!' he shouts. 'I'll be back on Saturday. Get to work!'

And before anyone can say anything, he's thrown his BOSS pass at me, and slammed the door shut behind him.

The whole office is pressed up against the

window in panicked silence, watching Pop Griffin stomp out of the building then roar away in his bright red Rolls Royce.

I can only see the backs of their heads, but I can hear their voices quite clearly.

'Is this a joke?' says one.

'Is this a test?' says another.

'This is insane!' says Mr Jackson.

'This can't be happening!' says my dad.

And then each and every one of them – Angela, Tim, Mr Jackson, Dad, all of them – turn round. Their mouths are wide open, like shocked goldfish. One or two of them silently point at me.

Me.

Joss Pilfrey. Ten-year-old girl.

Their new boss.

CHAPTER SIX

I am absolutely buzzing with questions, but Dad is very quiet in the car on the way home. He is staring straight ahead and keeps shaking his head.

Every now and again he just suddenly says, 'UN-be-*LIEV*-able!' or 'I don't BELIEVE it!!!' I think he's pretty proud.

Me? How do you think I feel? Who gets

promoted right to the top on their very first day, when they don't even work for the company and are in fact a child? Has this ever happened before in the whole entire history of working professionals? I've only been there one day and I'm already making history!

I'm having too many ideas.

If Pop Griffin isn't back until Saturday at the very least, that gives me nearly a *whole week* to run the company! The things I could do!

I stare at my BOSS pass. It is the pass to ultimate power.

What would Mrs Bonney make of this?

I can open any electronic door I like with this pass!

I can take anything I want from the stationery cupboard, no questions asked!

Dad is still just open-mouthed and shaking his head. He's stopped muttering to himself

and is now making a sort of whimpering noise.
I start to worry that maybe it is not pride but
something else that he's feeling.

'The important thing,' I tell him softly, 'is
that you just keep treating me normally. Think
of me as your daughter. Don't think of me as
your boss.'

Dad grips the steering wheel really tightly.

'Well? How was it?' asks Mum when we get home. She's in the kitchen with a mug of tea, very relaxed, and for some reason smells strongly of coconut.

Dad charges straight past her to get to the fridge.

'It was *the perfect day,*' says Dad, but it doesn't sound like he means it. 'Pop Griffin has gone entirely mad.'

'Well, it was only a matter of time!' says Mum. 'He's always been a bit eccentric.'

'He put Joss in charge of the entire company.'

'Haha!' laughs Mum. 'Imagine that.'

'Oh, you don't have to imagine, I mean it!' says Dad. 'I've brought the new boss home for dinner, so we should probably tidy up.'

'Well,' says Mum, winking at me. 'I better be on my best behaviour. For *Joss the Boss*!'

Finally, some respect.

'Lorraine, I'm serious,' says Dad, throwing his hands in the air. 'Your daughter – who is TEN! – is now the latest person at Griffin Games to have been promoted instead of me!'

Mum slams her mug down, her face completely blank.

'What?'

'I think I made quite a good first impression,' I say. 'Tim and Kareem were bickering, and Barry didn't seem to understand what was going on. I was the only one to put my hand up. I tried to make Bob do it, but he was too scared.'

'I was not scared, I thought it was a *test*!'

Mum is making a really weird face now. She looks like a monkey trying to make sense of a tin opener. But it really is very simple: I impressed so much on my very first day thanks to my can-do attitude that I am now in charge of Griffin

Games and everyone who works there.

This will be a very important period in all our lives!

Dinner was awkward. Now that we're colleagues, Dad has gone very quiet.

'But she's a kid,' Mum is saying, almost to herself. 'There are rules. He just made a mistake.'

I understand how Mum is feeling, but the more I think about it, the more I do feel I deserve this promotion.

I showed real leadership putting my hand up like that!

The fact is, Mum's just going to miss me at school this week and all my many questions. By always being in her office, watching and questioning her, she has constant companionship that money can't buy. When I point that out to her, she suddenly changes her tune.

'Well, I mean, it *is* only a week or so,' she says, thinking out loud. 'And she'll catch up on schoolwork, I'll make sure of it. And what an experience it would be, taking charge of a whole company! What would you do in her position, Bob?'

'Exactly, Bob!' I say. 'It's the job you've always wanted! Your dream job!'

'And *you've* got it!' says Dad. 'Has everyone gone mad? Is it catching? Joss can't miss a week of school, it's impossible!'

He seems to think just by saying something is impossible, you make it impossible. Did they not say that about space travel? Did they not say that about the Big Mac?

'Well, it's not *impossible*,' says Mum. 'She'd need her head teacher's permission. But luckily . . .'

Mum smiles to herself. She is a good mum, making a sacrifice like this. How many other mums would do the same, knowing they were throwing themselves into a long slow week without me there to stare at her all lunch hour?

'Bob,' I say, 'I understand you're unhappy at how things turned out today. As your boss, your opinion is very important to me.'

Dad goes bright red.

'My door is always open,' I say, resting my hand on his.

'What is it you always say, dear?' says Mum. '"Grab every opportunity"?'

Dad looks flabbergasted. I think he needs some leadership, pronto.

'Now,' I say, tapping my watch. 'It's getting

late, and you've got work in the morning. Best start getting ready for bed.'

'It's quarter to seven!' he cries.

'You can read in bed for a bit,' I say.

Dad stares at Mum. Then he quietly tidies away his plate and goes upstairs.

CHAPTER SEVEN

I'm going to be honest with you. I found it very hard to get to sleep.

At first it was because I was so excited. The access to brightly coloured whiteboard markers alone was beyond my wildest dreams. But then I began to worry.

What if I don't do a good enough job once I work out what the job actually involves? What if my

colleagues don't accept my leadership? What would Pop Griffin do then? Would he really close it all down? Would I become not just Dad's new boss . . . but also his last one?

By the morning I'm not even sure I want to do it any more. I have brushed my teeth twice even though I don't feel like eating any breakfast.

I need to get a grip. I stare at myself in the mirror while I make my ponytail extra smart and say, 'you got this, Joss!'

I also take comfort from how happy Mum seems. She is whistling in the kitchen and seems as free as a bird. I have clearly inspired her.

Dad, on the other hand, hasn't even shaved yet. He's still in his T-shirt and pyjama bottoms and I don't think he's slept very well either.

I know what will cheer him up. A private meeting with the boss! How lucky he is!

I have absolutely no idea what I'm doing so I will just have to act the part.

'Will you be shaving soon?' I ask him.

'I'm having my breakfast,' he says.

'What you do in your own time is entirely your business,' I say. 'But tell me . . . what exactly is it you do at Griffin Games?'

He just stares at me. I think he's a bit worried. I get ready to write it all down on my clipboard.

'This isn't a formal thing,' I say. 'Your position is quite safe. I'm not thinking of firing you.'

Dad looks horrified. I should stop saying things like that. I should wait until he's at work.

'I just wondered because all I really know is that you have a messy desk and that sometimes you use the phone or your computer.'

It is amazing how little I know about my dad's job. I don't think I'd ever thought about it much before. It was just a place where he went while Mum and I take care of the important things at school.

'I am in charge of making sure we have enough of everything,' he says, with a sigh. 'So that when someone orders something from Griffin Games, we can send it to them, wherever they are in the world.'

'Hmm,' I say. 'That sounds like something a computer could do.'

'What?!' says Dad. 'Well, no, it's a little more complicated than that!'

'And which is your favourite of the Griffin Games games? Which one do you love the most or have the most fun with?'

'Well,' he shrugs. 'I don't know. They're all

just numbers to me. We don't sit about playing all day! Work is supposed to be work!'

'Interesting,' I say, just like Mrs Bonney does when someone gives an answer in class, and I add this to my list of things to raise in my own Big Meeting.

Because that's the one thing I know that they like to do at Dad's work so far. Have a really big meeting.

'Hello everybody!' I say as they start to arrive in the office. 'Happy Tuesday!'

I have been standing by the door for ages, waiting, with butterflies in my tummy.

I smooth down my purple jumper and make sure my shirt collar isn't tucked in. I rub my smart shoes against the back of my trouser legs, just to give them a little polish.

I think some of my new colleagues are surprised I'm actually here. But Pop Griffin told me to be. I am the wearer of the BOSS pass. Without me, there'd be no boss at all!

Most people are kind of ignoring me. They're all about twice my size and even though I'm wearing my BOSS pass they seem not to notice it.

Tim and Kareem come in squabbling and brush straight past me. I am sure they will come to respect me; they're probably just nervous around the new boss.

I remember on the first day of the school year, Mrs Bonney wrote her name on the board, and that was that: we knew she was in charge.

So I noisily drag a chair to the office whiteboard and stand on it, and write out my name:

JOSS
PILFREY

I have decided I'm not going to make them call me 'Miss'.

But no one even turns round.

'Hello everyone,' I say, but people are just picking up phones and sighing and dialling numbers.

I try waiting. But it doesn't work.

Some people are sitting down. Some have mugs of coffee. Some are nibbling on steak bakes. Others are rubbing their eyes, all tired.

It's time to act.

I walk over to the kitchenette. I open a drawer. I find a plate and a wooden spoon.

I walk back to my chair, stand on it, and BANG the plate three times.

And I shout, 'One, two, three – *EYES ON ME!'*

There is total silence.

All you can hear is the creak of office chairs as people slowly sit up, or the soft sound a phone makes as people gently hang up.

Then I quietly ask everyone standing up to sit at their desks, because I'm going to take the register.

You can see people thinking . . . *register?*

Yes. Register.

Dad had already told me all the names of the people who work in the office, and I have arranged the register in alphabetical order. I stay standing on my chair and clear my throat.

A few people are muttering and complaining to each other. Maybe they are wondering if this is all part of a clever test by Pop Griffin, to see how they'd react if he suddenly handed the company to a ten-year-old. But I am not just any old ten-year-old. I am a ten-year-old who has been waiting for this moment for a decade.

Mr Jackson looks very grumpy. He's been giving me Looks ever since he arrived. He's chomping away at an apple like he wants to destroy it. I think he thinks he's still in charge. It is important I show my authority immediately, just like Mrs Bonney showed me.

Angela is first on the register and I call her name.

'ANGELA!'

'Yes?' replies Angela quietly, like she hates speaking out loud.

'Are you here?' I ask.

'What do you mean?' she says. She looks like

she thinks she's done something wrong.

'I just mean, are you here today? Are you here at work?'

'What?' she says.

'It's for the register,' I say, tapping it. 'We're doing the register! Are you here today?'

Angela starts to panic.

'I think so?' she says. 'I don't want to get this wrong!'

Maybe she is worried because I am the new boss and she wants to please me.

'This isn't a test, Angela,' I say. 'I just want to know if you're here or not. Can you tell me if you're here or not?'

'I'm here,' says Angela. Then she says, 'I'm sorry,' and she gets up and runs to the toilet.

I see Mr Jackson rolling his eyes at her.

I am going to have to keep my eye on Mr Jackson.

CHAPTER EIGHT

After the register, I used Dad's phone to make a bell ringing sound, and then signalled that people should begin their work.

They were actually really respectful of that. They got their heads down and began immediately. I have decided my first day as boss will involve lots of observing. Only by observing will I know what to have a Big Meeting about.

Mrs Bonney does lots of observing at school. Once she's set us a task, she will sometimes slowly wander round the room looking over people's shoulders. Sometimes she'll say something encouraging like 'that's nice' or 'well done' to someone like Sarah, or if she's not happy she'll get someone to do something all over again.

And so that's what I will do next. It is the best way to get to know the strengths and weaknesses of my employees. I start with Barry.

'And what do you do here, Barry?' I ask.

'As little as possible!' he says, and then starts laughing.

I do not laugh.

'No, I, um – I just try and keep my head down,' he says. 'Keep out of trouble.'

Hmm.

I move on to Dad, who sees me coming and sighs as he puts his phone down.

'What would you say is your greatest weakness?' I ask.

'Um . . . I would say my greatest weakness is that I'm a perfectionist,' tries Dad. 'My weakness is that I just never stop until something's perfect.'

'That doesn't sound like a weakness,' I say. 'That sounds like a strength. Maybe your weakness is you don't understand questions properly.'

Dad's face goes bright red. He keeps avoiding eye contact with me, shuffling papers on his desk and acting like I'm not there.

I stand really close behind him. He's writing an email so, in order to encourage him, I loudly point out every time he has made a spelling mistake. He can spell perfectly well if he takes his time, but the more I do it, the more he starts rushing and typing things wrong.

'*Der* Eric?' I might say, pretending to be confused. 'Do you mean *Dear* Eric?'

I notice Dad's shoulders tremble every time I do this, which is a lot.

'Don't be nervous,' I whisper, leaning into his ear. 'You're doing *really well*.'

On the whole, I am pleased to tell you that behaviour in the office seems excellent. No one seems to even look at, or talk to, anyone else. There's no chit-chat. Nobody laughs. No wonder Dad loves it here.

And – best of all – there's the stationery cupboard. A whole cupboard packed

THE STATIONERY ♡ CUPBOARD! ↘

with all the very best treats imaginable: four-colour biros, paperclips in sensible silver and brass, glorious navy blue holepunches and more staples than you could ever imagine. I have definitely landed on my feet in this job.

Unusually, though, there is nothing on the walls. No name cards on the desks or plants to take care of. They don't even have an office pet! If someone disappeared, I don't think you'd even notice. It is very different from my classroom. How do grown-ups know when they've achieved something good? How do they know where to sit? Or where they belong? Where is the sense of pride?

And then something surprising happens. As I walk between the desks, with my hands behind my back, I can see Mr Jackson giggling with Barry and Fiona. They're laughing along. And they're certainly not working.

I get a little scared. I know I should say something. I am the boss. For a moment I consider pretending I haven't seen, but then I remember Mrs Bonney.

So, I do what Mrs Bonney does. I stand in complete silence with my eyebrows raised and I just stare at them.

Stare at them *hard*.

But they just carry on, giggling and chatting.

I don't feel quite brave enough to make a fuss because they're grown-ups and they know each other but if I don't say something they might act like this all day.

'Is everything okay, Mr Jackson?' I ask, trying to make my voice sound strong. I should go on to say something like 'do you want to share it with the group?' but my mind goes blank.

'Everything's fine, kid,' says Mr Jackson. 'Come on, guys.'

He walks towards the door, with Barry and Fiona trailing obediently behind him.

'Where are you going?' I ask.

But they don't even answer. They just walk out, Mr Jackson waiting for Barry or Fiona to hold the door open for him. I hear them laughing and high-fiving, and their squeaky shoes on the hallway floor.

When I look out of the window, the three of them are leaning against a wall in the car park.

Fiona is drinking a Coke and Mr Jackson is expertly throwing a rolled-up ball of aluminium foil from his sandwiches straight into the bin. He has loosened his tie and so has Barry. They glance up at me and Mr Jackson smirks. I think he is a very bad influence. And he's eaten his sandwiches far too early. I look at my watch. It's not even breaktime at school yet!

And that gives me an idea that I write down on my clipboard.

'What is the best thing about working at Griffin Games?' I ask Angela.

I think it's important to ask Angela questions and get her to talk a bit more. I appreciate her quiet work ethic, but I think she might be lacking in confidence.

'I don't know what the best thing is,' says Angela, looking a bit startled. 'The steak bakes? I usually eat at my desk.'

'You eat at your desk?' I say. 'Why?'

She looks a bit shy to tell me, but Mr Jackson bursts back into the office, laughing with Fiona and Barry. He is talking really loudly and Dad has to put a finger in his ear so that he can keep speaking on the phone.

'Indoor voice, please!' I say, striding up to them, and Fiona scuttles off.

But Mr Jackson just keeps talking to Barry and laughing. He is talking *at* Barry very loudly and obnoxiously about the day he won a football game. He is using words he shouldn't be using in an office environment and in front of a child, even if that child *is* the boss.

'Mr Jackson,' I say sharply, but I don't think my sharp voice works, because then Mr Jackson says, 'Ssh, can you hear that? It sounds like an annoying fly.'

WHAT??!! *He is talking about ME.*

'Um, Joss,' says Dad. 'Can I have a quick word? Right now?'

I see what he's trying to do. Dad's trying to protect me by getting me away from this situation. But I have to stand firm. It's what any good Class Monitor would do.

'Mr Jackson and Barry,' I say. 'Am I going to have to split you two up?'

Barry looks guilty, but Mr Jackson looks straight at me and says, 'Off you go – *little girl.*'

UGH!

Mr Jackson is really horrible.

First off, he has ZERO respect for authority. Even if he disagrees with a ten-year-old being his boss, he needs to think about Pop Griffin's wishes. He needs to Respect the BOSS pass!

And he seems quite lazy. He never even got that stockroom door fixed!

I totally see now why Dad was so annoyed that Mr Jackson got the promotion and he didn't.

After Mr Jackson called me a little girl I didn't know what to say, so I just turned round and walked off, keeping my head high. Dad asked me to sit with him for a bit while he made some calls, but I'm sitting in the toilets now, and even though I'm trying to be a professional and boss-like, I feel really stupid and small.

Just like an annoying fly.

Especially because straight afterwards, Mr Jackson made a big deal of walking round the office, checking on people's work, probably because he saw me do it earlier. He had a right go at Angela, and then even at Fiona and Barry, telling them all the things they'd done wrong.

That's *my* job! He thinks he is still the boss, not me. And because everyone is unsure about it, they let him be.

I need to do something.

It's then that I hear something from the other cubicle. It sounds like someone trying not to cry.

I don't know what to say. The person on the other side of the cubicle doesn't know I'm here and I don't want to embarrass them. Being a grown-up seems both very boring and very stressful. Apparently, you're either in a grey-walled office or the toilets. That's no way to live.

But then I have a great idea.

CHAPTER NINE

'Okay!' I say, holding up Dad's phone and making the bell sound again. 'Everybody outside at once!'

Immediately people start SCREAMING.

'Fire!' yells Barry. 'It must be a fire!'

'No!' I shout, but it's too late, people are jumping up from their desks in a panic. 'No, it's not a fire drill!'

'What, then?!' screams Fiona.

'It's breaktime!' I say, delighted.

I have personally never been a huge fan of breaktime. I think it disrupts the flow of a good school day. But there must be a reason we have them.

'Breaktime?' says Dad. 'What do we do in breaktime?'

'We have a break!' I say. 'Everybody into the car park!'

But there is another reason I'm doing this, too.

'Great, a break,' says Mr Jackson, sarcastically, as he reaches for his coat. 'What a childish idea.'

'Not you, Mr Jackson,' I say. 'You already took your break, even though you didn't ask properly. You and Barry and Fiona can stay inside and carry on with your work.'

Mr Jackson looks furious.

'But everybody else is getting a break,' Fiona says, looking genuinely sad.

'That's right,' I say, crossing my arms. It is very important I seem strong and in charge. It will send a message to the more disruptive people.

'Come on, Angela,' I say, 'let's get some fresh air! Bring your fruit if you like!'

From the car park I look up and see Mr Jackson, Fiona and Barry glaring out of the window. Everyone else is down here now, standing round and looking confused.

'Run!' I tell them, encouragingly. 'Be free! Enjoy yourselves!'

I wave my arms around to make them move, the way you'd try to move a swan or a big ostrich or something.

But all the grown-ups just sort of look at each other. Where is their imagination?

'Isn't there a game you want to play?' I ask. 'You could play tag.'

But no one seems very keen. It is very odd that you never see grown-ups playing tag. Or manhunt. Or hide and seek. I know that I don't like playing things like that but the other kids sure do.

'It's quite cold,' says Angela. 'We should probably get back to work.'

'Fresh air is good for you,' I say. 'Helps clear the mind. And don't you have any healthy snacks or anything? Tomorrow, I want you to bring snacks. Fresh fruit and water. Not fizzy drinks and chocolate.'

People begin to nod. Maybe since they saw me stand up to Mr Jackson, they are taking me a little more seriously.

'It's just that there's not much to do out here, in this car park,' says Tim. 'And like Andrea says, it's quite cold.'

Andrea? Her name is *Angela!* I've only been here a day and even I know that.

I realize that although all these people go to the same place every day, they don't really seem to be friends.

Do these people not know each other at all?

When we got back into the office, I sent Dad down to the basement to fetch a Griffin Games all-weather outdoor ball, and he came back with a glittery one that had a unicorn on it.

'There's actually some great stuff down there!' he says when he returns. 'I haven't been in there for ages. I used to spend hours in there. Sometimes I'd choose you a new ball like this one, when you were younger.'

'Perfect!' I say, taking the ball. I look at all the people I've arranged on seats in a circle by the photocopier. 'Now, when I throw the ball to you, I want you to say your name out loud and an interesting fact about yourself.'

This is an old trick Mrs Bonney used to do, especially when new kids joined our class. She calls it the Team-building Ball. It is a great way to learn names and find out about each other. Griffin Games definitely needs a bit of that.

I throw the ball to Tim.

'I'm Tim,' says Tim, awkwardly. 'And my interesting fact is that I am learning karate.'

'Oooh,' say a few people and Tim blushes.

He throws the ball swiftly to his left.

'I'm Kareem,' says Kareem. 'And actually, my interesting fact is that I am *also* learning karate.'

Tim didn't seem to know that. He gives Kareem a small nod.

'You could be karate buddies!' I say. This is working perfectly! 'Kareem, who's next?'

Kareem throws the ball to Mr Jackson, who makes catching the ball look really complicated so he seems brilliant at catching balls.

'You all know who I am,' he smirks, arrogantly. 'And you know I have a very interesting and varied life. But I guess if I had to choose just one thing, it would be that I am going on a very expensive holiday to Antigua next month – probably the most expensive one I've ever been on – and I'll also be upgrading my car again soon. I just can't decide whether to go for the convertible or the one with the Batman doors.'

Everybody makes super-impressed faces.

Mr Jackson lobs the ball high into the air.

It bounces on the floor and lands in Angela's lap.

She doesn't look happy about it.

She thinks for a moment.

'I'm Angela,' she says, staring at the floor. 'And I don't know what my interesting fact about me is.'

She looks ready to throw the ball to someone else, but I say, 'Come on – there must be something!'

Angela looks a bit awkward, but I don't want her to not do this.

'I used to have a very beautiful dog,' she says, sadly, and then throws the ball.

Lots of people have brought Angela a cup of tea to make her feel better. She now has six cups of tea lined up on her desk. She also has a mountain of biscuits, and even though they're not very good for her, I will turn a blind eye.

CUPS OF TEA

BISCUITS

'When we have important news,' I told her after the ball game, 'it's good to share it with people.'

That's what Mrs Bonney told our class after Jack Davis's grandma got ill.

'That way people will know a bit more about what you're going through.'

I'm watching from a distance, as people who used to just walk past her desk stop and ask Angela about her dog and whether she has any photos of him. Just then Dad puts his hand on my shoulder.

'That was actually really good, Joss,' he says.

I smile but then realize he's away from his desk.

'Back to work, Dad. I mean, Bob.'

He grins at me then shuffles back to his messy desk.

I really think I'm onto something with this whole team-building thing. Thanks for that one, Mrs Bonney.

At the end of the day, it feels like everyone has done lots of work. I tell them I won't be taking it home to mark because I trust them, but also because I don't think bosses do that, actually.

'Tomorrow,' I say, 'I want each and every one of you to come in wearing purple and yellow.'

'Oh,' says Fiona. 'For charity or something?'

'No,' I say. 'Just a new rule.'

And when everyone else (apart from me and Dad) had gone home, I headed straight for the stationery cupboard.

CHAPTER TEN

The next morning, all you could hear was people saying, 'Wow!' and 'Ooh!'

Dad and I had stayed late last night. I told him if he helped me, I'd secretly make him the Boss's Number One Assistant, and he rolled his eyes but accepted.

First, we'd stapled loads of old pieces of paper from the recycling bin onto the walls. I'd drawn

a giant picture of Kareem and Tim in karate gear and written PUNCH YOUR WAY TO PROFIT! and FIGHT FOR GRIFFIN GAMES!

I also made lots of other highly inspirational posters and wrote the motivational slogan of the day across the whiteboard. Plus, I put pretty purple and yellow Post-it notes up everywhere. Just like at Twin Pines, those were going to be

our colours. That way, if you saw someone in purple and yellow, you'd say, 'They work for Griffin Games!' Well, either that or you'd think they went to my primary school, but that's unlikely if the person you see is forty-seven.

I'd also drawn out a big timetable that I put on the wall. There is a good reason why schools have timetables and I see no reason why adults get away with just doing whatever they feel like whenever they like.

'So, breaktime is now a permanent fixture, is it?' Mr Jackson scowls, looking at my colour-coding. 'So, every morning we just stop working? The whole place just shuts down for a bit, does it? I don't think Pop Griffin is going to be too happy about that. I'm certainly not.'

I have a brilliant breaktime planned today, but we'll get to that.

'You look like clowns wearing those colours,' says Mr Jackson who has grumpily turned up as if it's non-uniform day in his boring grey suit.

'I think we look very smart,' says Tim.

'Oh, be quiet, Tim,' spits Mr Jackson.

But Tim's right – they do look smart. Even though some are in shirts and others are in jumpers and some are in dresses, the colours mean they look . . . like a *team*.

Elsewhere on the timetable, I've colour-coded lunch at the same time for everyone. And we're all going to eat together. I have put one person in charge of teas and coffees each day because it's better to have a Tea & Coffee Monitor than loads of people randomly running around making drinks all the time. It also makes sure that no one misses out on having a drink or gets the wrong mug.

I have loads of great ideas to get Griffin Games back to the top of the class again. But my favourite one is this . . .

At breaktime, I tell everyone we're going down to the car park again.

I'm pleased to see that when I started to speak, they all put their phones down like good boys and girls.

Of course, I know they all think the car park is cold and pretty boring, on account of it just being a big concrete space with some cars parked in it. Yesterday they said they had nothing to do there, so I have something special prepared for them today. I remembered what Dad said about Griffin Games just being numbers to him these days. Well, how could they make and sell these games if they didn't know if they were fun or not?

As you know, I don't normally have much time for fun and games, what with all my many school responsibilities, but I have looked at the statistics online and most people enjoy both fun *and* games. It's unbelievable how many.

When we get downstairs, Kareem is the first to spot what I've arranged.

'No way!' he says. 'That's awesome!'

It's not just a car park any more. It's a *play* park.

'There's a helter-skelter!' shouts Fiona.

'Yes, Fiona! And a giant bell to ring!' I add.

There are things to bounce on, run on and jump on.

Balls everywhere. Hula hoops. And now there is a bunch of grown-ups running towards it all and shrieking with glee, as they see all the Griffin Games bestsellers Dad and I have brought up from the basement.

'I want first go on the helter-skelter!' shouts Tim, and he runs up the stairs, getting ready to slide all the way down again, which makes you wonder why he bothered in the first place.

But it is nice to see the grown-ups getting some

fresh air and exercise. You need to tire adults out a bit. Get their blood pumping. I think we'll see some really good work getting done a bit later on. That's what I'm counting on anyway.

The only person who isn't joining in is Mr Jackson. He's skulking off to one side, scrolling on his phone. He keeps looking at me and then looking away. I should really confiscate the phone, but I suppose it is breaktime. I wonder who he's calling? Maybe he wants his mum to pick him up.

I see Kareem bouncing up and down on a roll-out piano mat, stamping out some terrible music. Two other people are playing frisbee, and even Angela is jumping on the mini trampoline. Sleepy Ken appears to be passed out on an inflatable armchair.

'Joss! Look at me!' yells Dad, bouncing round on a space hopper. 'Wheeeee!'

I look over at Barry having a go on the Swingball. He's huffing and puffing and even though he keeps missing the ball, he's clearly having a great time. I'm actually quite tempted to try to dig out the one Dad brought back home for me, but then . . .

'Excuse me,' says an old lady, shuffling by the car park entrance with her little Scottie dog. 'How old are these children?!'

'A little older than you might think!' I say.

'Aren't they having fun!' she says. 'Nothing better than running around in the fresh air! You know, there used to be a small park here many years ago. My husband and I would sit on the bench and listen to the children play. It's so nice to hear the laughter. I could listen to it all day!'

'Oh, me too,' I say proudly.

And then I blow on my whistle. Break over!

CHAPTER ELEVEN

Well, you would not believe the noise back in the office.

As soon as we're inside, phones are picked up, people are jabbering, emails are whooshing, and everyone is incredibly busy.

'You have GOT to install one of our Griffin Games helter-skelters!' Fiona is telling someone on the phone. 'We've just been out on ours and it is EPIC!'

She pauses.

'You'll take TWO?!'

She gives me a big thumbs up, and I ring our new Sell Bell. That's what I've decided the bell from outside should be.

THE SELL BELL

Every time someone does a good job on something, I give the old Sell Bell a whack to let the whole place know. It is my version of the Well Bell, I suppose.

Mr Jackson is still on the phone in his private office. He is glaring at me from behind the glass. Finally, he hangs up and shakes his head in disgust.

But this is *good*, right?

Tim has decided to completely change

the Griffin Games website. It used to be a really boring big list, with loads of words and tiny images, but now he's making it all really zingy – as colourful as our office now is. He's even using the videos he made of everyone having fun in the car park with silly captions. He definitely gets a GREAT WORK! sticker today.

'I just sold three Giant Chess sets and an Inflatable Volleyball Court!' yells Barry, and I ring the Sell Bell four times.

Everyone cheers! That's another GREAT WORK! sticker right there!

This is exactly why I should have been made Class Monitor. I am some kind of business visionary.

'PUNCH FOR PROFIT, KAREEM!' I yell, doing karate chops in the air. 'FIGHT FOR GRIFFIN GAMES!'

At the end of the day, my colleagues tell me they have never sold so many things in one afternoon. Or had so much fun. Or got so many stickers.

In the corner of my eye, though, I see a sticker-less Mr Jackson on his phone again.

When we get home, Dad seems quite tired and quiet. He must just be exhausted, poor thing. It was a big day. Not only did he run about all breaktime, but I think he worked harder than he ever has before.

'So, what happened today?' asks Mum, as Dad plonks the spaghetti down on the table. 'Tell me all about it.'

'I invented the all-at-once Office Breaktime,' I say, 'because people were just taking breaks willy-nilly and as you know, fresh air, exercise and healthy snacks are very important. I also started a dress code so that the employees of Griffin Games understand that they are a team and are ambassadors of the company. Plus, I made motivational posters and gave everyone a deeper understanding of the products they sell.'

Mum looks stunned.

'Wow,' she says. 'Anything else?'

'I thought back to my days at nursery and I'm considering bringing in nap times for some of the older employees. There is a man called Sleepy Ken and I think he needs it.'

I look over at Dad, who still looks wiped out.

'Tough day, Bob?' says Mum. 'Were you on your best behaviour for the new boss?'

Dad smiles but stays quiet. He and mum share one of those Looks that I never understand.

I'm worried I've done something wrong.

'You can say if I've done something wrong, Bob,' I try. 'I promise there won't be any professional repercussions.'

Dad lifts a forkful of spaghetti and snorts.

'It was one of our most profitable days ever,' he says, though not very happily.

I frown. Mum frowns. But that's good, right?

'Why didn't I ever suggest any of those things?' he says with a shrug. 'How come it took Joss to do it?'

I remember Mum say that Dad's confidence took a real knock when the company brought Mr Jackson in. Mum was always encouraging Dad to stand up for himself or take the initiative to try different things. Mum's always been really strong that way. It's how she became a head teacher and got her very own office. But Dad always said there was a way that Griffin Games liked to do things and Mr Jackson said you weren't allowed to do them differently, so why even try?

That does not sound like grabbing every opportunity at all to me.

I'm supposed to do a whole bunch of homework to catch up at school, plus Mum says I need to do some chores. But now that I am a boss, I feel a bit beyond all that. Besides, being a boss is exhausting.

Maybe I can delegate some of that stuff to Dad. Do you know the word 'delegate'? It means when you get someone else to do something you don't want to do. Dad half-heartedly tries to put up a fight, but I subtly stroke my BOSS pass and he soon falls into line.

'Make sure you use a ruler for the drawing

of the pyramids because Mrs Bonney is very strict about that,' I say. 'And Mum expects those knives and forks to be stacked in the dishwasher just the way she likes them.'

Dad is not happy about the latest tasks, but these are the perils of living with your boss. And this is great time management on my part. Because even though I am absolutely wiped out, I still have something quite important to do for work before bedtime. And I will need access to Dad's contacts book . . .

CHAPTER TWELVE

Day three! Wednesday! Everyone at the office calls it 'Hump Day' because it's the middle of the week and it's like getting over a hump. I call it Hump Day because it really feels like Mr Jackson has got the hump and will never let it go.

He's skulking around after register and putting people off. So, I give the staff a motivational speech, praising them for all the cracking work they did yesterday.

And I announce the Griffin Games Star of the Week Award – a new scheme I came up with last night while I was in the bath, a bit like what we did at my school at the end of the summer term last year.

Sarah won 'MOST THOUGHTFUL' and Mohammed won 'FUNNIEST', but I was happiest, because I won 'KID MOST LIKELY TO RUN THE SCHOOL ONE DAY'. I mean, *that's* an award. The Griffin Games Star of the Week Award will unite and inspire!

I also decide to ask them to all sit on the floor in front of me because every day we're going to do some reading to get us in the mood.

THE GAME OF LIFE
The secrets of my success
POP GRIFFIN

I have chosen Pop Griffin's autobiography, which is published by Griffin Books, and is called THE GAME OF LIFE: The Secrets of My Success.

I am amazed no one here has ever read this before. Not one of them!

I start with the first chapter of three hundred. It is entitled 'Every Single Detail of My Birth'.

When the nurse first saw me that famous day, she said, 'I believe this child will start a great business one day, he will start a great business!' and do you know what? She was right, she was — she was right! I'll never know how she knew, no, I won't know that. Perhaps it was because I had a very straight back, a determined grin and I never ever cried.

I could tell they weren't very interested in this bit. A few of them started yawning.

I skipped ahead a hundred pages.

Then, on my second day, I was given my first briefcase. It was a leather one with a silver lock and I named it Samson.

I decided that I needed to make it a bit more interesting and make a few things up.

So anyway . . . right after that I decided to start Griffin Games and make it the coolest, best place to work! Because the lesson I learned that day as a baby with a briefcase is that ANYONE can be a baby or have a briefcase. But only SOME people get to work at Griffin Games! A place where every idea matters! Which is why we've got to get out there today – and sell, sell, SELL!

'Yes!' shouted Angela, which was very unlike

her and afterwards she came up to me shyly.

'I've drawn a new sign,' she says. 'It's for where we get the mugs.'

Normally the sign there says USE YOUR OWN MUG! because grown-ups seem to be really weird about other people using their mugs instead of sharing them like families do. It appears to be some kind of crime to use someone else's mug. I really need to get my own BOSS mug.

'Show me,' I say, and Angela holds up a piece of paper, no bigger than a Post-It note.

It says, 'You're Doing Really Well!' and there's a picture of a mug, smiling.

'Angela, that is *brilliant*,' I say.

'Really? You don't have to say it is if it's not.'

'I'm going to photocopy it and put it everywhere,' I say, and she blushes.

'I didn't know whether it was stupid,' she says shyly, 'but I thought people might like it.'

Angela looks a bit different now. It's like her back is straighter, like she's grown taller overnight. I noticed earlier she brought in a framed photo of her dog, the one that passed away. It sits on her desk and gives her comfort.

I have an idea.

'You've been working here ages, haven't you? How would you like your own special project?'

'Ooh,' she says, looking nervous. 'Me?'

At breaktime, I am supervising again.

Barry is back on the Swingball. He's clearly

been practising, because today he is absolutely brilliant at it. No one can beat him.

'Um, Joss?' says Tim. 'Can I ask you something?'

Tim says he was thinking about what I said about every idea mattering. He says he might possibly have an idea for work, but then he gets all nervous about saying it out loud.

I tell him if he's worried, he can write it down and give it to me. I remember Mrs Bonney once telling us that if we're having trouble saying something out loud, sometimes it helps to write it down.

'You can make it real that way,' I say, 'but in your own time.'

Tim looks a bit happier, and I tell him I very much appreciate the extra effort he's putting in.

'Thanks,' he says. 'We don't normally hear any nice things about what we do.'

'Oh,' I say, spotting Mr Jackson on the other

side of the car park, drinking a Coke and still not joining in. Fiona is standing next to him and she looks desperate to use the helter-skelter but I guess Mr Jackson has had a word with her.

'Mr Jackson never tells us if we're doing well,' says Tim. 'He only says if we're doing badly. My wife says he wants to keep us nervous, so that we'll just be grateful to have the job.'

Harrumph. That is terrible!

'Every time we come up with a new idea, he just says "no, that's not how we do things here".'

That's *just* what Dad said about Mr Jackson.

Suddenly I notice the old lady with the little Scottie dog is back.

'Off you go, Tim!' I say. 'Go and play!'

'They grow up so fast,' says the old lady, smiling as Tim runs off to find a ball.

'Don't they,' I say.

'They're like dogs!' she says. 'You've got to tire them out.'

I enjoy grown-up humour. It's not very funny, but it is friendly.

'I'm Maude,' she says. 'You must struggle looking after so many of them!'

'Do you know what,' I say, 'they're generally very well-behaved. And I'm Joss, by the way.'

'Well, seeing them have fun is such a tonic, isn't it, Baxter?' she says, smiling at her dog.

'Come on then, we'll see Joss and all the children again tomorrow!'

I watch her walk away very slowly. She looks like she has a sore back. I hope someone's looking after her.

CHAPTER THIRTEEN

After lunch, which we all ate together in the office, I notice some of the staff are a little noisy, probably because they've had fizzy drinks. Kareem is laughing loudly as he tells Dad a funny story about a karate kick he did. To calm them all down, I read another inspirational chapter from Pop Griffin's book. We're on chapter sixty-seven, which is called 'Lessons I Learned as a

Toddler', and then I clap the book shut and make an announcement.

'You are all doing really well,' I say, and I notice Tim and Barry and Fiona all smile with pride. 'But I feel like you grown-ups don't really get enough feedback.'

Barry puts his hand up.

'Yes, Barry?'

'We do get a performance review every now and then,' he says, and everybody groans. 'They tend to be quite sad times.'

'I wonder why,' says Mr Jackson, rolling his eyes.

'And I bet you get all moody about it,' I say. 'Then you go home and say you had a bad day at work and nobody understands why, because they don't know much about your job.'

'Yes,' says Barry, and Mr Jackson frowns at him. 'My son doesn't really know what I do. He just tells the other kids at school that I'm an estate agent.'

'Not everybody can be an estate agent,' I say. 'The world needs . . . er, what is it you do again?'

'Accounts administrator.'

'Well, the world needs accounts administrators, I imagine, so it's about time they find out just how great you are at accounts administrating!'

I have no idea what I just said but it sounded good.

I absolutely love parents' evening at my school. Even though Mrs Bonney is hardly likely to say anything bad about me because my mum is her boss, it is important that other people see how you're doing so they can be proud of you.

'So,' I say, holding up a spreadsheet I made last night, 'I've invited some of your family members in so that I can tell them what you're like at work.'

They all look absolutely horrified.

'I'm not sure that's a good idea!' says Kareem.

Why not? I think. Kids have to do it – all the time! And why wouldn't they want their kids and husbands and wives and partners to sit down with their boss and hear all about their strengths and weaknesses as they just sit there silently?

'It will be FINE!' I say encouragingly.

'Bob,' says Mr Jackson, speaking over my head to Dad. 'Can I have a word?'

Dad glances over to me, obviously asking for permission.

'Okay, but don't be too long,' I say.

I let Mr Jackson talk to Dad privately in his office. They say you should keep your friends close but your enemies closer, but I didn't do it because of that. I did it to show I am a considerate boss. It is good to give people a little independence and trust them. And also Dad will totally tell me what Mr Jackson says, because he's *my dad*. We're a team, even though I am definitely team leader.

'So, here's that idea I had,' says Tim, a bit nervously, handing me a piece of paper with some very imaginative art on it. 'It's Kareem's as well. It's probably rubbish. I'm sorry for even giving it to you.'

'Thank you, Tim. It's nice to see you working with Kareem. Now back to work, please.'

He bounces off and picks up his phone.

When Dad gets back from talking to Mr Jackson, I say, 'What was all that about?'

And he says, 'Oh, nothing. He's just a bit worried about you inviting people's families in without telling them. He says you should keep work and family separate.'

'Oh,' I say. 'What do you think?'

Dad looks sheepish.

'I mean, I suppose I can see his point.'

What does Dad mean by that? He can't really be agreeing with Mr Jackson – but . . . he's not disagreeing either. I'm a bit worried that Dad means me – that maybe he secretly thinks that I should be kept separate from his work? But no, of course not. I am proving to be an excellent boss and Dad knows that. And anyway, he always says 'Grab every opportunity' and this is me grabbing with both hands! I think he's just nervous about Mum coming in, in case she sees him staring at his screen all day, or she finds out about the steak bakes and says he's got to have fruit instead.

I can't help but feel there's something going on. Is Mr Jackson up to something?

CHAPTER FOURTEEN

At 5 p.m., the first of the family members start to arrive.

I have given Barry and Fiona special name badges I made myself and positioned them by the office door. I feel like by making them the welcoming party, it might show them how nice it is to be part of things – rather than always being led astray by a bad apple. Barry is very enthusiastic and shows people all the phones we use. Fiona is pointing out all our inspirational posters and signs. Her husband pats her on the back and says, 'You're really talented, Fiona!' and she blushes with pride.

Everyone looks really impressed and the compliments are flying.

Maybe I should also do report cards. Grown-ups don't seem to get them. Why? I love report card day. It is the one time I really get to celebrate.

Anyway, it's time to get down to business.

First up is Mrs Jackson and the three Jackson children. I show them my BOSS pass as they sit down across from me, because it's important to show identification, but also because I'm showing off a bit.

THE JACKSONS

Each of the Jackson children is wearing the same fancy tracksuit, and Mrs Jackson is dressed up like she's going to the opera.

I begin as positively as I can.

'Well, first of all, Mr Jackson is a really engaged member of the company,' I say.

'Oh, that's nice to hear,' says Mrs Jackson, 'because we do worry about him.'

'Cynthia!' says Mr Jackson, sharply.

'Do you?' I say. 'Yes, I can see why.'

Mr Jackson is scowling.

'Sometimes,' I say, like it's a secret, 'I do think his attitude could be a little better. He often gets a little distracted and can be a bit disruptive.'

Mrs Jackson says 'Stephen!' and gives him a look. The Jackson children snigger.

'But if he can manage to apply himself, I'm certain he'll do really well.'

'This is ridiculous,' says Mr Jackson, with a sour face.

'Thank you for the feedback, Joss,' says Cynthia. 'I think the kids and I could do with one of those BOSS passes at home!'

Mrs Jackson takes Mr Jackson's hand and leads him away.

Next up is Angela. I managed to get her sister, Ruth, to come in, and she takes a seat next to her.

'So, Angela is a little quiet at work and I just

wanted to make sure everything was all right at home?' I ask.

Ruth nods. 'Oh yes,' she says. 'Everything is fine. She's getting better and better at cooking. Last night she made a chicken curry all on her own from scratch.'

'Angela!' I say. 'That's fantastic! You should have brought some in to show us! Maybe we'll do a Show and Tell and you can bring in your curry.'

'I think she's cheered up a bit these last few days,' says Ruth. 'Apart from, well, you know. Missing good old Rufus.'

I make a sad face. She must have loved that dog.

'Well,' I say, 'the good news is, Angela's work here at Griffin Games is terrific. I even gave her a special secret project. I don't know what she was like before, but I think she's really coming on!'

Angela's face brightens.

'She just needs to have a little more confidence in herself. But I've been really pleased to see her getting on so well with everyone and joining in.'

I think the thing with Angela is that it's very important I don't damage her confidence. I hope I never did that with Sarah. Maybe what I don't say is just as important as what I do.

'So, it's top marks from me!'

'Well done, Angela!' says Ruth, and Angela smiles. It is just a small smile, but it is an important one – because I think it's the first smile of hers I've seen.

Then I do Kareem and Barry and Fiona and all the others, but I've saved Dad for last, because I still need him to get my lift home.

Mum sits down and smooths down her skirt. She looks rather amused.

'Now, Mrs Pilfrey,' I say, trying to keep things formal. 'As you know, I'm a big fan of your husband and think he has bags of potential.'

'Thank you,' says Mum. 'We like him.'

'Now I've had to be a little bit strict with him lately because it's important not to have favourites. Generally, there's nothing to worry about, and I've even secretly made him my Number One Assistant. But I am a little worried because he sometimes gets distracted and I catch him looking out of the window daydreaming about steak bakes or sneaking off to make another coffee where he likes to gossip with the other workers.'

'I don't daydream!' says Dad, and Mum gives him a smile.

'Don't interrupt Joss when she's talking,' she says softly. 'He can be a bit like that at home, to be honest.'

'*Can* he?' I ask.

'Mmm,' says Mum. 'He's been promising to

fix one of the radiators for ages, but he keeps getting distracted and forgets.'

'Oh dear,' I say. 'Well, Bob, I hope I don't have to take away any of your computer time.'

'How would I do my work if you did?' says Dad.

'*Bob*,' says Mum. 'Don't be so cheeky. I'm sorry, Miss Pilfrey, he's not usually like this.'

And then there's this moment where I stare at Dad and Mum stares at me and Dad stares at his shoes, and we all realize how crazy this whole situation is.

And we start to laugh. For absolutely ages.

At home, we were still laughing about the fact that I'd given Dad such a good report.

'It's all about who you know!' he kept saying.

He'd also asked if getting such a good report

meant he could get a treat for being such a good worker, and Mum had said we could pick up hamburgers on the way home.

'I'm pleased you're having such a nice time at the office, Joss,' says Mum, putting the burgers and fries on white plates because she thinks that makes them look healthier. 'I know I'm always trying to get you to do what the other kids do. But I guess everyone has fun in their own way and I should encourage that.'

'Thank you,' I say. 'But also . . . does anybody know where my old Swingball set is?'

Mum and Dad beam at each other.

'I do!' yells Dad.

Out in the back garden, Dad starts lunging and stretching. He looks very competitive.

'Now you understand that if I lose, it's only because you're my boss and I'm letting you?' he confirms.

'Oh sure,' I say. 'You have to let the boss win, that's the law.'

He smiles and whacks the ball. It zings round and round and none of us manage to hit it and we're so bad it's *hilarious*.

'That looks fun,' says Mum, bringing us some ice cream.

Part of me wants to say I'm just researching a Griffin Games product so I can understand it better, but that's not true. This *is* fun. Fun for the sake of fun is . . . fun.

'It's a lot quieter at school without you,' says

Mum, as I grab the ball and hit it towards Dad. 'There's certainly more time to fill. You are definitely someone you notice is missing.'

I think that is the nicest compliment I've ever had. But it makes me think of someone else and I stop the ball for a second.

'How's Sarah doing?'

'Sarah with the red gloves from your class?' asks Mum.

'Yes, that's her. It's just . . . There's someone at work that really reminds me of her, and it's made me think I need to try a bit harder to be nicer to her.'

Mum's face softens. 'What do you mean?' she says.

'Well, I'm always trying to inspire Sarah by showing her how I do things but maybe that's not helpful. I've always thought she was quiet, but I've never thought to find out why.

Some people need help to make them feel a bit better about themselves. I'm trying to do that with Angela, but I wonder if I do that enough with Sarah. Maybe we need to do more things *together*.'

Dad senses an opportunity.

'Would you . . . would you like an afterschool hang-out with Sarah?' he asks. 'I know you'd probably prefer a trip to the pen shop, but maybe you could play Swingball with her in the garden? Or I could take you to the cinema? Or bowling. Biking. Climbing. Anything. Or you could just run around in the park?'

'I'm sure there'll be *something* fun, Dad,' I say, letting go of the ball and whacking it. 'But first, I still have two days of work left . . .'

CHAPTER FIFTEEN

Thursday begins mysteriously, because Mr Jackson is absolutely nowhere to be seen.

Everyone notices. I must have said his name ten times when we did the register. I knew he wasn't there, I just wasn't sure what to do next so I just kept saying 'Mr Jackson?' to try and buy myself some time.

After about thirty seconds of this I decided I

had to say something else. So, I drew a big line through his name and made a disapproving face. Everybody knew he was in trouble now.

'Right,' I say, moving on. 'There's something I'd like us all to do this morning.'

Sometimes when it rains at school, we have indoor play. I usually really like that, because I can sit at my desk and get some extra work done. But I heard about these companies in America that let their grown-ups play at the office, too.

'We've got a ball pit!' yells Kareem, delighted. 'And a slide to slide into it!'

Oh yes.

BALL PIT!

'Ball pits have been shown to encourage co-operative play and increase social skills!' I say. That's something they can tell our customers! 'But it's also just really fun.'

I also brought up a big play tent, for Sleepy Ken. It turns out that he's got three babies at home. Maybe he just needs a good rest in that play tent so he can finally do his work properly.

Now we've also got inflatable skittles and a bowling ball, which I thought people could use when deciding whose turn it is to empty the recycling bin or refill the photocopier. And I've brought up soft play mats, a Swingball and an easel, in case anybody fancies designing new games.

You've never heard a louder office! Partly because I've swapped all the boring grey keyboards for light-up LED gamer ones that are *very* tap-tap-tappy. But also because everyone is whooping and high-fiving and everything is great, until the door swings open to reveal a very unimpressed Mr Jackson.

'Ah, Mr Jackson, nice of you to join us,' I say sarcastically.

'I'm here, aren't I?' He sniffs. 'Are you all having a nice *play*?'

Everyone is looking at me, not sure if they're allowed to keep going.

'Do you have a note or anything, Mr Jackson?' I ask.

'From who?' he asks, angrily. 'My mum? I'm forty-three and head of sales. No, I just didn't fancy coming in on time. I *decided* to be late.'

I know exactly what he's doing. I've seen kids at school do this. They're challenging authority.

'Take your seat and I'll have a think about what to do,' I say.

'Ooooooh,' says everyone else, in a very dramatic way.

All day Mr Jackson behaves very badly. Distracting others. Whispering to people. Telling them not to go in the ball pit. I even catch him whispering to Dad. What is he up to? Is he really that embarrassed about not getting a good report? I did try to give him constructive criticism, but it feels like he is doing the opposite of everything I suggested!

I am seething, but I am also a bit scared. I have no idea how to punish him, but I know I am going to have to, because otherwise he'll think he can act like this every day.

Should I phone his wife again and tell her how naughty he's being? I wish I could send him to sit outside Pop Griffin's office, but that would be pointless as everyone knows he's out on his boat.

And then I realize what I have to do. I'm going to handle this head on.

I take a deep breath and I stand up in front of the whole office, and I say, 'Mr Jackson – see me, please.'

Three terrifying words. *See. Me. Please.*

A hush sweeps across the room. Mr Jackson is ignoring me. I might also have to take five minutes off his breaktime.

'Mr Jackson?' I try again. 'I said "see me, please".'

Mr Jackson pretends not to hear me. He picks up a book and starts to read it.

I don't want to have to do this. But he made me do it. I'm going to use *every tool in my arsenal.*

'Stephen *Simon* Jackson,' I say. 'One, two, three – eyes on me.'

There is a gasp in the room.

But Mr Jackson does nothing.

'I *said*, one, two, three – EYES ON ME!'

Nothing!

Mr Jackson leans back in his chair, exhales, and puts his feet on his desk.

The cheek!

'Would you put your feet on your furniture at home?' I ask crossly.

'Yes,' says Mr Jackson. 'I've got a foot stool.'

Barry laughs out loud, then puts his hand over his mouth guiltily.

'Well anyway, I've had a think about what to do about your attitude . . .' I say, trying to come up with a punishment, '. . . and I'd like you to work from *home* tomorrow.'

Imagine not being able to fully enjoy the benefits of an office!

'Work from home?!' he says, shocked.

'Wait . . . are you *excluding* me?'

Big gasps everywhere! Open mouths and wide eyes!

I suppose I am. Maybe sitting at home will give him time to think about his behaviour.

I don't know what else to do. So, I think I should change the subject! Reward some *positive* behaviour, just like Mrs Bonney does.

'Tim and Kareem!' I yell. *'See me, please!'*

Tim and Kareem look absolutely terrified, like I'm going to set them extra homework or something, but I am doing this on purpose.

'I'm shouting because I'm excited!' I say, holding up the piece of paper Tim gave me yesterday. 'This is a great idea!'

Tim and Kareem beam at each other.

I catch Mr Jackson's eye. He is staring at me, absolutely furious.

CHAPTER SIXTEEN

Tim and Kareem have asked to start an afterwork club. I am more than happy to give it my approval. It's called 'Kareem & Tim's Karate Klub' and, before it starts, they both get changed into their karate uniforms in the toilets. They have the headbands and everything.

'Come on, Barry, let's get out of here,' says Mr Jackson, looking at Kareem and Tim with a

sneer. 'Are you coming, Fiona?'

Barry and Fiona look a little sheepish.

'I guess so,' says Fiona, sadly.

'Fiona and Barry,' I say, hands on my hips. 'If Mr Jackson told you to jump off a cliff, would you?'

They stare at their shoes and say 'No'.

'So, if you want to do karate club, tell him you want to do karate club.'

'I think they can speak for themselves, kid,'

says Mr Jackson. 'Just wearing a BOSS pass doesn't mean you can . . . boss them around.'

Er, yeah, it does. But that's not what I'm doing.

'Mr Jackson,' I say, 'you better be getting home, from where you will be working tomorrow.'

'We want to do karate with Tim and Kareem,' says Fiona quietly, still looking at her shoes.

'You're not serious?' says Mr Jackson. 'Well have fun, you karate *nerds*. I'm off for a steak bake and then I'm going to drive round in my car listening to music really loud and then tomorrow I'm going to get up late and not do any work until eleven o'clock.'

'I'll expect you to call me at ten,' I say.

'FINE!' he screams, and he flounces off. I see him throw a horrible look at my dad. They stare at each other for a little too long as he goes.

'Don't listen to Mr Jackson,' I say. 'Outside interests are very important. They make you

149

a far more rounded individual, and karate club will look great on your CV if you ever want a new job that requires hand-to-hand combat.'

I have to say, Kareem and Tim have made a great start with their club. They've managed to get half the office signed up, and they're using our Griffin Games mini trampolines to do their jump-kicks before landing on Griffin Games crash mats.

'Are you going to have a go, Miss?' asks Kareem, not realizing he's just called me 'Miss'. 'I'll teach you how to karate chop!'

'We really have to head home, I'm afraid,' says Dad, covering for me.

Dad's right. I shouldn't really, it might seem unprofessional . . . but, oh gosh, it does look fun. Everyone's excited about joining in. Sometimes I do wish I was more like the other kids. I mean, I'm perfectly happy being me, but I'm just one person. Maybe it would be more fun if I was not just me on my own.

'Anyway, have fun everyone,' says Dad.

'Wait,' I say. 'Actually, *can* I, Bob?'

Dad looks at me, confused. I'm asking his permission because, well, he's my dad.

'You're the boss, Joss,' he says with a tired grin.

So, I take off my sweater and my pass and pull my socks up, and soon I am bouncing through the air, doing roundhouse kicks as everyone cheers.

'Like this!' says Kareem, and he bounces so high his head touches the polystyrene ceiling, and he spins through the air and lands brilliantly.

Fiona has a go, and even though she splits her trousers on a super high kick, she is beaming.

Then I bounce, and leap, and spin, and land, and I feel great. I feel confident and strong!

'Haai-YA!' I yell, and now even Sleepy Ken cheers, but that's because he's just woken up

151

at his desk and he doesn't know what's going on. He must think he's woken up in a martial arts film.

Although I am quite sweaty when it's finished, I have to admit, it really is a great bonding experience.

'Let's have more afterwork clubs!' I say. 'Everybody come up with an idea and have it on my desk in the morning!'

'Yes, boss!' they shout.

'Home time now?' asks Dad. 'I've still got to finish your pyramid project tonight. I should be asking for overtime pay, really, you know!'

I go to get my stuff, and I pull on my sweater, and put my pens back in my pocket, and look for my BOSS pass.

'WAIT,' I say, suddenly very worried and confused indeed.

Something terrible has happened.

'I must have misremembered,' I say when I get home. 'I thought I took it off before karate, I'm *sure* I did, but maybe I wasn't wearing it today?'

That would not be like me at all. And I do remember taking it off after work, I know I do.

'Have you checked your room?' asks Dad.

I run upstairs to make sure it's not magically on my bed or something.

'It's not here!' I wail. I can't believe it.

I've lost my BOSS pass. What kind of a boss loses their BOSS pass?

I run outside and check in the car yet again. Then I check my pockets for the five hundred billionth time. I can't stop patting myself in case it's somewhere – anywhere – my BOSS pass, my responsibility, my power.

Dad comes in when I'm in bed. He says I should get an early night and we'll look in the morning. I feel sick. What am I going to tell Pop Griffin when he gets back?

Dad strokes my hair gently.

'Everything happens for a reason, J,' he says. 'It might even be for the best.'

He doesn't feel like my employee any more. He feels like my dad. I'm grateful for him telling me it'll be okay, that maybe we can find a new one or something, but I just feel like a kid again. A kid who wasn't careful enough, and who did a stupid karate class when she should have gone home like a proper boss. I lie in bed in the dark with tears in my eyes.

And at first, they're sad tears.

But soon they become angry ones.

It just feels like something really unfair has happened to me, and I don't know how, or what to do about it.

You see! This is what happens when you take your eye off the ball and have 'fun'! This is what happens when you join in.

I wish I could talk to someone. Someone like me, who'd understand.

Instead, I plump up my pillow and try and go to sleep.

CHAPTER SEVENTEEN

The next morning, Friday, was supposed to be my most triumphant one. And yet here I am, sitting at the breakfast table, unable to eat because I'm so worried.

Where could my BOSS pass have gone? Did someone . . . take it?

And of course, I couldn't help but think what you're probably thinking right now:

Mr Jackson did it.

I'd ignored the idea because I couldn't believe someone in a position of authority would ever do such a thing. But the more I thought about it, the clearer it was: Mr Jackson *must* have something to do with this. He's been on me since day one. He didn't like anything I did. He didn't even want me at Griffin Games in the first place. But stealing or hiding my pass was a very serious thing to accuse someone of. I would have to keep my theory under wraps until I could prove it.

Anyway, it's just a pass – I know I can make my own. And surely I've done enough to show my authority at Griffin Games. We have made such good progress!

But I notice Dad hasn't cleared away his plates from the table, and he knows I prefer a clean space in the mornings.

'Bob, do you want to tidy this away, please?' I say.

'In a minute, Joss. We *are* still at home, you know,' he says, not looking up at me.

Oh, gosh, it's started already. I feel my authority draining away.

Mum is more reassuring.

'Think back to where you were when you last had your pass,' she says. This is typical grown-up advice. If I knew where it was when I last had it, I'd still have it! 'But remember – you don't need a pass or a title to be the boss. A good leader just leads. You just *are* the boss, Joss.'

But that's not true, is it? At school, I'm not Class Monitor. I wish I was, but I can't just say I am. You have to be made it. And that pass was my proof I'd been *made boss*.

Still. At least Mr Jackson wouldn't be there. He'd be at home, stewing away, kicking himself for being so rude. At least that was some comfort. It would buy me some time to work out what to do next.

At work, I can't help but feel like something has immediately changed too. It's probably just me being paranoid, but as I walk in, it seems so quiet. Does everyone know already?

I can't help it, I keep tracing my finger round my neck, hoping I'll suddenly find the BOSS pass there again. No one looks up to greet me. Everyone is just quietly tapping away on their computers. We're a little late because Dad said we should have one last look for my pass this morning.

I keep hearing quiet *dings* as emails arrive.

'Morning, everybody,' I say lightly, and one or two people look up and smile back briefly.

'How was everyone's evening? Were you all tired after karate?'

I hear another soft *ding* and everyone continues clicking and typing again. And is my memory letting me down, or have some of my motivational posters disappeared?

'Um . . . has everyone had a coffee or a tea?' I say, looking at the monitor chart on the wall. 'I believe it's Fiona's turn today?'

Fiona looks at me guiltily.

'We're not allowed to do that any more,' she whispers. 'We all got an email from Mr Jackson this morning. He says he's been on a Zoom call with Pop Griffin and things have to go back to how they were. He says Pop Griffin was furious, hearing about the changes, and about how you lost his BOSS pass.'

I go bright red. I feel so ashamed and silly.

'Mr Jackson says Pop Griffin is getting ready to

come back RIGHT NOW,' says Fiona, 'and if we want to keep our jobs we have to do as he says.'

I must look like I'm going to be sick, because Fiona says, 'Sorry, Joss, you did your best,' and squeezes my arm.

I do what feels natural and walk to Dad. As I do so, I notice a few people taking off their yellow or purple jumpers and putting them to one side.

'Dad,' I say, when I get to his desk. 'See me? Please?'

'Joss,' he says softly. 'Why don't you take a break? Let me see what's going on. I'll have a read of the emails. You go and get some air.'

'I can wait until breaktime,' I say.

'I don't think there's going to be a breaktime any more,' he says. 'Sorry, sweetheart.'

But everybody loved breaktime! And my posters! This is all horrible.

Everything is going wrong.

CHAPTER EIGHTEEN

Outside, I sit on the wall in the car park and lick my wounds.

Stupid Mr Jackson. Just because one day a kid was made his boss. What was his problem? Things like this must happen every day!

I must be scowling because I hear a voice saying, 'Cheer up, it might never happen!'

It's Maude, the old lady, and her Scottie dog.

'I'm afraid it did just happen,' I say. 'I'm on the scrap heap. I've been demoted. On my last day.'

'Well, never mind,' she says, leaning her shopping trolley against the wall and sitting down next to me. 'You seemed very good at your job to me. The way you handled all those big children, running round and screaming all the time.'

'Funny thing is,' I say, 'they're the adults. I'm only ten.'

'Ten?!' she says. 'I thought you were about forty! Really must get my eyesight checked again. Well, I don't think you can really be on the scrapheap if you're only ten. Surely you should just be having fun?'

'That's what my mum always says,' I tell her,

'but I'm the sort of kid who finds responsibility fun. And now I've had it all taken away from me. Next week I'll go back to school, and I'm scared because time is running out and soon I'll be at secondary school and I won't know how to be. At all.'

Wow.

I'd never said that out loud before.

I don't even think I'd truly realized that's what I was scared of.

At Twin Pines, see, I know what I'm doing. That's probably why I do so much of it. I don't want it to end. I have a very good relationship with the head teacher. I have used my time well, built up a reputation, earned my stars. At a new school I'll have nothing and no one.

'Changes are hard,' says Maude. 'I'm supposed to make a big change soon.'

'A new job?' I ask.

'No,' she says, with a chuckle. 'I mean, I'm eighty-four.'

She's probably retired.

'No, there's a new phase I know I need to get ready for, just like you. But I'm scared too.'

Maude tells me she's got a little too old to look after herself all the time. Her knees hurt and her back hurts, and she lives in this big old house down the road, on her own, on Thomas Street. She says the only reason she doesn't want to move into a place with carers is because they won't also look after Baxter. Pets aren't allowed, even though he's not a pet, he's one of the family. Her best friend. She says even though there will be people around her, she might feel even more alone without him. Plus, she'd have to sell her house, and it's in such a terrible state. The garden is overgrown, the door needs painting, the windowsills are peeling. It's all a bit too much for her.

'So, you see, everyone has things they're worried about,' she says. 'Everyone is worried about change, because when something changes you feel like you can't control it. I guess the answer is, try to accept the change but also make sure you take a little control of it for yourself somehow. But people aren't always brave enough to do that.'

And she pats me on the shoulder, throws Baxter a treat from her pocket, and slowly walks away.

Well, I better get back to work.

But when I get to the door, I realize I can't get in. It's locked. And my BOSS pass is gone so I can't swipe the keypad.

I ring the buzzer, but everyone must be busy, because no one answers.

And when I turn round, my humiliation is complete. Mr Jackson is stood right behind me!

'Having trouble?' He smirks. I notice that as usual he is wearing neither purple nor yellow.

'Have you seen my BOSS pass, Mr Jackson?' I ask pointedly. 'Only I had it last night around the time you left.'

'You still had it when I went home,' he says innocently.

I thought back. Was he right?

Yes, he was. He'd left, and then I'd taken my pass off to get ready for karate. So, was it my fault after all, then? Did I just lose it? Did I leave it behind like it didn't matter to me?

'Luckily I still have mine,' he says.

He holds up his own pass. It is not a BOSS pass, but he clearly thinks that because he has a pass and I don't, he is in charge. He swipes it on the keypad and the door clicks open.

'You're not supposed to be in today,' I say, walking in quickly so he can't lock me out. 'You're supposed to be working from home.'

'Yes, well, things change,' he says. 'And it turns out I don't take my orders from you. Never mind, Joss – *these things happen.*'

THESE THINGS HAPPEN?!

I am seething now.

'Wait,' I say. 'How did you know about me losing my pass? Like you say, you'd already left when I took it off.'

'A little bird told me,' he says with an infuriatingly smug grin on his face, pressing the button for the lift.

A little bird?! A SPY! I have heard of this. They call it industrial espionage. Someone has been working with Mr Jackson to outwit me.

But why? Who would do such a thing?

Maybe it was Barry, after all. He's always right there, near Mr Jackson, isn't he? Maybe he didn't like playing Swingball as much as I thought he did. I suspect he wants an easy life and that's the best way to get it.

And now I know one thing for sure – I didn't lose my pass.

My pass *was* stolen!

CHAPTER NINETEEN

Everyone keeps their heads down as Mr Jackson and I walk into the office. We are both trying to walk normally but at the same time get ahead of each other. Being in front shows that you are in charge. But it means we have to take really quick little steps, so we both end up looking like irritated penguins.

Mr Jackson seems taller than ever. His

charcoal grey suit has been ironed. I bet he even ironed his socks for today.

'Okay, people!' shouts Mr Jackson. I can't let him do all the talking, so I stand on a chair and say, 'Right, people!'

'We're going to get back to work!' says Mr Jackson, and I quickly yell, 'It's work time!'

Everyone is looking confused because they don't know who to pay attention to.

'Some of Joss's ideas were okay but misguided,' Mr Jackson says. 'I like motivational posters, so I'm putting my own up.'

He signals to Barry – the SPY! – who starts taking the rest of my happy colourful ones down and replacing them with signs that say:

and

and

Barry is a traitor, I'm sure of it! I give him

exactly the type of look you give a traitor or a spy, and he almost quivers.

And Mr Jackson can't resist showing off his power. His evil plan has worked, and he's lording it up as if I was never a boss in the first place. Somehow, I need to prove it was an evil plan. But I already feel defeated. He and Barry will just deny it all. I feel small and stupid and I want to cry.

'Seeing as you're still here, Joss, I do have one job for you,' says Mr Jackson. 'It's in the stockroom. I'm afraid there are no windows and there won't be anyone to talk to, but you can spend your last day here down there.'

I look to Dad, who gives me a sad look in return. He's mouthing at me: 'It'll be okay.'

But I don't think he knows that for sure.

I was feeling very sorry for myself, but the stockroom is not so bad really. There is a tiny office with a desk. And plenty of filing cabinets, so if you like filing cabinets (like I do) it's pretty cool. And I suppose at least down here I'm in charge of something.

I look around. I am boss of that big bin over there. And the small fly buzzing round the lightbulb? I am its superior. I suppose I could make some changes down here. I could fix that door, couldn't I?

I think about the sign I saw that started all this.

REMEMBER TO USE THE DOORSTOP IN THE STOCKROOM OTHERWISE YOU WILL END UP LOCKED IN THERE FOR EVER. I should have fixed it when I had the chance. When I had the power.

Instead, Mr Jackson wants me to go through loads of old paperwork from the 1980s and put it all in alphabetical order. He didn't say why. The stack of paper must be taller than Dad!

Poor Dad. He's still up there, having to work for Mr Jackson again. He must be feeling completely miserable right now. For a while Dad was truly living the dream. His own

daughter was his boss. A child! Able to wield her kind power over him and give him a Gold Star sticker every now and again. Imagine how proud he must have been! I forgot that he must have been just as devastated as I was when my

BOSS pass disappeared. He must have been so sad, knowing that in that moment I had lost all authority over him. That I wouldn't be able to boss him around, not just at work but at home too. He is also a victim in all this.

Barry has a lot to answer for. I am so disappointed in him. I thought I could trust him. But all along he'd been hiding that his true loyalty was to Mr Jackson. Probably just so he'd get a promotion or something.

A promotion my *dad* deserves! My lovely, loyal dad.

Yes, big bad Barry must have stayed behind at karate and secretly hidden my BOSS pass when no one was looking.

But that doesn't make sense, because Dad would have spotted him, and Dad would have told me what was happening. That's what a Boss's Number One Assistant would do.

I'll ask Dad before I accuse Barry.

After all, Barry was busy doing karate chops. Wasn't it actually me who encouraged him to stay after work and do it?

And Dad was standing right there by my clothes when I got changed into my karate outfit. He'd have definitely stopped Barry from stealing my pass. Dad wouldn't let Mr Jackson win. Come to think of it, Dad was next to the BOSS pass the whole time.

Dad was the closest one to it.

Dad was the only one near it!

. . .

Wait.

CHAPTER TWENTY

The first thing I notice when I get back upstairs is that there is a very tense atmosphere. People don't seem happy sitting under their shouty new posters. Mr Jackson is pacing around, keeping his eye on everybody, like it's an exam or something.

'You are not a team,' Mr Jackson is saying as he walks around. 'You are individuals. You cannot rely on each other. You can only rely on me. Only listen to ME.'

He really seems to be making up for lost time. It's like he is trying to get people to forget everything they learned this week.

I notice Tim getting annoyed at Kareem, and Angela looks like she wishes her computer would swallow her up.

And my worst fears are confirmed.

Dad's desk has moved. Now it's right outside Mr Jackson's office!

I almost had to put my hand on the wall, I was that shocked.

Could it really be true that my dad – my own father! – had taken and hidden my BOSS pass? Just so he could suck up to Mr Jackson and get ahead in the company? At his own daughter's expense?

I didn't want to have to do this, but I couldn't help myself. This was a *saying-someone's-full-name* situation.

'Robert John *Pilfrey*,' I say sternly. 'You are in big trouble, young man!'

Why is it that saying someone's full name out loud has such power? Mrs Bonney doesn't do it much but when she does it's like the whole world stops.

Dad turns to me, looking very guilty indeed. Oh, I have caught him in his little game. And I honestly cannot believe he has put me in this situation. My Number One Assistant, of all people!

'Bob – *Dad*,' I say, with my hands on my hips. 'Can I have a word in private?'

But Dad has a new protector.

'You can chat in your own time,' says Mr Jackson, standing up from his desk. 'Please don't distract my employee from his work.'

'It is important,' I say.

'Back down to the stockroom with you, Joss,'

says Mr Jackson. 'Oh, and I've called your school to say they're to expect you back on Monday, after Pop Griffin gets back and sees that I have shown my initiative and rescued this company from your silly ideas.'

'They weren't silly,' I say, and I look round for someone who'll agree with me.

Fiona?

Kareem?

Tim?

Barry?

But none of them can meet my eye.

'Having a breaktime and playing on a helter-skelter in the car park isn't silly,' I say, but as I do, I start to lose faith. 'Making posters isn't silly. Letting Sleepy Ken have nap time in an office tent isn't silly. I don't think rewarding good behaviour is silly. Wearing team colours at work isn't silly . . .'

And as I continue, I start to realize that I'm making it all sound silly.

'Swingball isn't silly. Um, karate club isn't silly.'

But now it's me that feels silly. These people were at work. They're just supposed to turn up, tap at their computers, make some phone calls and go home again. I was treating the whole thing like it was supposed to be . . . fun. As fun as school!

But maybe I've ruined everything. Maybe I've made things worse for them. I certainly seem to have got them into trouble with their real boss, while I was playing pretend boss.

Dad seems to want to tell me something. I think he wants to say sorry. But I don't want to hear it. I thought I was doing something good. I thought we all were.

'Everyone needs to work late tonight. You all need to make up for the wasted time this week,' says Mr Jackson.

'But it's Friday!' wails Kareem.

'And I want everybody in tomorrow, too!' says Mr Jackson.

'But . . . but that's *Saturday*!' protests Fiona.

'Well, I'm pleased you know your days of the week,' says Mr Jackson. 'Saturday is just another day. And Pop Griffin wants us all here when he gets in.'

'All of us?!' panics Angela.

'*Everybody*. We've got a lot of catching up to do. There'll be no more silliness. No more "bonding". Just paperwork, coffee and even more paperwork.'

Everybody groans.

Mum came to pick me up and take me home.

I ate my pesto pasta in silence while Mum kept asking me what had happened and why I was so upset. She was getting really worried and blaming herself for letting me spend the whole week at Griffin Games. I was only ten, she kept saying.

I still couldn't tell her. Not yet. I kept picturing me doing my best karate kicks, and Dad quietly picking up my BOSS pass. His eyes darting around to make sure he wasn't being watched. Throwing it in the bin or hiding it in a filing cabinet. Keeping it a secret from me, even as I panicked.

In the end I had to tell her. Mum's eyes widened and she took a deep sigh.

'Sometimes, Joss, people do the wrong thing for the right reason. And that can be really hard to understand,' she says. 'But you mark my words, I think it will all turn out for the best.'

But I didn't have the energy to mark her words. I was too sad, and just went to bed, and pretended to be was asleep when Dad popped his head round the door at about midnight.

CHAPTER TWENTY-ONE

Saturday morning rolled around, and I really didn't want to go to Griffin Games, even though Mr Jackson had said 'everybody'. If I didn't turn up it would be just another excuse for him to make me feel bad.

I wanted to hide. And I didn't want to speak to Dad.

But I could hear him down at the breakfast

table talking with Mum. She was asking him whether it was really true Mr Jackson was going to make him start working more weekends.

Working *weekends*? That was *so* Mr Jackson. I can't imagine anyone would be happy about that. Working weekends is in my opinion a crime against humanity. Particularly now that everyone was into helter-skelters and outdoor games. Sleepy Ken likes walking in the park with his babies in their mega stroller on weekends. Tim and Kareem have signed up for karate weekend retreats. And Dad . . . well, he sometimes takes me to whatever the hot new museum is on weekends. Or helps with my homework. Or snores really loudly on the sofa.

'Bob,' I say coldly as I walk into the kitchen. Mum glances at Dad and then quietly leaves the room.

'Hey, Joss,' he says immediately. 'Look, it's not what you think.'

'Oh, and what do I think, Bob?' I say pompously. 'That you needed me out of the way, so you stole my BOSS pass to get close to Mr Jackson?'

'Well,' he says. 'Yes, I did do that. But it's not like that . . .'

Busted! The cheek of the man!

'You worked against me with Mr Jackson!' I say.

'Just hold on a minute, Joss, he told me if you "lost" your BOSS pass, things would really change around the office . . . and I realized he was right.'

'Dad!' I say, outraged. 'Why didn't you tell me?'

'I promise you I did it for the right reasons.'

'The right reasons? Ha! You were jealous of

how well I was doing and you thought you could get a promotion!' I point out.

'No, that's not it at all!' says Dad. 'Joss, you made me realize that even if I had got that promotion, I'd never have done the job as brilliantly as my own daughter. You taught me loads about thinking differently!'

'Then why hide my BOSS pass and not tell me?'

'Listen, I wasn't sure my plan would work. I didn't think you'd let me try. But I saw an opportunity – and I grabbed it!'

An opportunity for himself! Thanks, Dad!

'Look, it's better I don't just *tell* you but *show* you.'

What's he going to show me? His promotion? A new friendship bracelet he's made for his best pal, Mr Jackson?

'Time is running out,' he says. 'Pop Griffin is

in today and we need to be there.'

And then, like something from an action movie, he puts his hand on my shoulder and says, 'Let's get to work, boss.'

I don't know what to expect. Dad is all jittery but in a confusingly good way.

'So last night was a *nightmare*,' he says, as we drive through town. 'The whole office started bickering and getting really annoyed with each other. Everyone was really hungry and ratty. Tim got so annoyed with Kareem he threw his stapler out of the window.'

'What?' I say.

'Some people were using words they should *not* be using. Mr Jackson totally lost it! He kept shouting at everyone and then storming off to his private office. And they were all so annoyed about him making them come in today! He couldn't make anyone get on with their work last night!'

Didn't he know the silent technique? Didn't he know how to say people's names in full? Could his mouth be incapable of saying 'One, two, three – *eyes on me!*'?

'People were so overtired and frustrated. No one was helping anyone else, because Mr Jackson kept saying we weren't a team, or that we were rubbish. Hardly anyone is talking to each other any more,' says Dad, beaming. 'It's worse than it ever was!'

I don't understand. Dad seems actually quite pleased about this. But doesn't he see? Everything I was trying to do as a boss was finally bringing them together. And by getting me put in the stockroom, he's undone all that!

'It was our least profitable Friday *ever*,' says Dad, and then he starts laughing out loud, and drumming the steering wheel with his hands, like that's a good thing. 'It was a disaster!'

He laughs even harder.

I begin to worry that now I'm no longer Joss the Boss, he's become Dad the Mad.

But something about it is exciting. And I realize that although I don't quite understand what's going on yet, if I trust my dad it'll be good.

And that maybe that strange glowing feeling in my chest might just be hope.

CHAPTER
TWENTY-TWO

The minute we get to the office, I see exactly what Dad means about it being worse than ever.

Everyone looks exhausted. My colour-coded timetable has been ripped off the wall. There are more awful posters saying: NO TALKING! and WHAT WOULD MR JACKSON DO? and YOUR DESK IS NOT YOUR DESK – IT IS THE COMPANY'S DESK SO KEEP IT CLEAN! They remind me a bit, I'm ashamed to say, of the ones I used to put up at school. I wouldn't do that any more. Obviously, Mr Jackson is trying to crush everyone's spirit as quickly as possible, so they do whatever he says!

'Kareem, I need those figures now,' says Tim grumpily. 'Hurry up.'

'You'll get them when you get them, Tim,' replies Kareem, not even looking at him.

I wish I was still in charge. I would take them to one side and make them say three nice things to each other until they realize they're best friends again.

I see five people walk past Angela's desk without even bothering to say hello. I notice the photo of her dog has disappeared.

No one is working together. Can't they see they're all on the same side? Maybe if they were wearing their uniforms again they'd understand better.

'Do you see what I mean?' says Dad, nudging me. 'It's a *very* different place from when you were in charge.'

It certainly is. And suddenly, it makes me feel really annoyed. All my good work was for nothing. It makes me realize I have a choice. I either walk away and let Mr Jackson win – or I try and save the office!

'WHY DO I HEAR TALKING?' yells Mr Jackson, opening the door of his office. 'Oh, Joss. I might have guessed it would be something to do with you. I'm actually impressed you showed up today – you show some gumption that your dad clearly lacks. Well, if you're here, then down to the stockroom with you.'

And that's it. I see red.

He starts to close his door, but I call out . . .

'Actually, Mr Jackson, there's a big problem with the stockroom.'

'A problem? All you have to do is sit there and put bits of paper in a pile.'

'It's actually pretty serious,' I snap. 'It involves all sorts of serious things. It's very important. You really need to come and look. Otherwise Pop Griffin might get really angry with you when he gets in later.'

I watch as he considers this, with my heart leaping in my throat. Dad looks at me, confused.

'What is it, then?' asks Mr Jackson, as we get out of the lift in the basement. 'What's so important that you've dragged me all the way downstairs to this horrible place?'

'It's all in there,' I say, and I stoop down to wrap my fingers round the little orange doorstop. 'Go inside and I'll show you what happens.'

Mr Jackson sighs and walks into the stockroom.

'What is it?' he says.

'It's this doorstop,' I say as I yank it out from

under the door. 'If someone's holding it when the door closes, the person in the stockroom gets locked in! Watch, I'll show you!'

'Noooo!' yells Mr Jackson, as the door swings shut in his furious face.

I've caught Mr Jackson! He's stuck in there!

'Joss! JOSS!' I hear him shout, all muffled, and he tries the handle a few times.

'Don't worry, Mr Jackson!' I shout. 'You stay there! I'll go get help!'

Back upstairs, Tim and Kareem are really arguing and stabbing angry fingers at each other. Fiona is yelling that someone's used her mug again. Angela is practically burrowed under her desk because she can't hear her phone call properly. Dad is sitting on the edge of his desk, watching it all, smiling, thoroughly enjoying the chaos.

'One, two, three – *eyes on me!*' I shout, clapping my hands together. Then I stand there on my chair with my eyebrows raised until everybody is quiet. 'I am not angry, but I am *very* disappointed. You have let me down. You have let Griffin Games down. But most importantly, you have let *yourselves* down!'

Everybody is just staring at their shoes.

'What happened to working together, praising each other, rewarding good behaviour?' I ask. 'It's obvious what we need to do before Pop Griffin gets back.'

'Resign?' says Kareem.

'No!' I say. 'A team-building exercise!'

'But, Joss,' says Dad looking aghast. 'If Pop gets back and sees the office in chaos, he'll know it's because of Mr Jackson!'

So that was Dad's big plan? He wanted to show Pop Griffin what a bad boss Mr Jackson was by making him see how unhappy everyone was when Mr Jackson was in charge? But that would mean they had to be unhappy. I would rather see them . . . happy.

'There are some things in life that are more important than getting credit for someone else doing a bad job, Dad,' I say. 'And we're about to do one of them now.'

CHAPTER
TWENTY-THREE

Out of the office we streamed, in a line at first and then as an excited bunch.

'Office team outing!' yells Kareem. 'Let's get hamburgers and go to a soft play!'

'We're going to do something much better than that!' I say, and I can feel the grin on my face getting wider and wider.

'What's that thumping coming from the

basement doors?' asks Angela, looking back at the building.

I say, 'Oh, that's nothing. Right. This way!'

Maude, the old lady, had told me she lived in Thomas Street, and when we got there, it was not hard at all to find her house.

It was the one no one had touched in years.

While every other house was quite smart and freshly painted, with fancy cars and burglar alarms, Maude's was just as she'd described.

The front garden was wild and overgrown. The door was old and dirty and might once have been yellow. The paint on the windows was peeling, the garden gate was hanging at an angle, the rubbish had piled up down the side. The shed had seen better days, and there were old, cracked flowerpots and wilting weeds all over the place.

'This is our "team-building" exercise!' I say, as people gather around me in the garden. 'We will learn to work together again and we will do something good! This is the home of the old lady who sometimes walks past our office.'

I take a deep breath and say: 'This is Project Maude!'

I clap my hands together and start to delegate roles.

'Tim and Kareem – you're on flower duty. I want bright flowers everywhere! I want those old flower beds dug up and some hanging baskets. And that trellis on the wall needs re-attaching and things growing up it. Jog down to the garden centre and get shopping!'

'Yes, Joss!' they say.

'Barry – you mow the lawn. Angela, those windows need a lick of paint! Check the shed for brushes! Fiona, sort out the rubbish! Dad, you're on weeding!'

'Aww, why do I get the worst job?' wails Dad.

'Because at home you sometimes make me pour out the bin juice and that's called "revenge". And Sleepy Ken?'

I look around.

'Where's Sleepy Ken?!'

'Um, he's back at the office,' says Tim. 'He's asleep.'

'Okay! Well, then I'll fix the gate with a screwdriver and polish the front door and see if it's yellow!'

Maude would be out on one of her daily walks with Baxter right now. She'd probably be shuffling past the car park wondering if those massive children were ever going to come out again. Maybe she wondered where I am too.

At Thomas Street, we got to work. Everything we needed was in Maude's shed: paint, brushes,

rakes, spades, soil, lawn mower and plenty of other things that hadn't been used since 1982.

We dug and painted and mowed and polished.

We painted and primped and primed.

We cleaned the windows and stopped the gate from squeaking.

And you know who was great? Barry. Nothing was too much trouble. He used a tiny pair of scissors to get the edges of the grass just right. He used the world's smallest scraper to help peel old paint off the windowsills. He took such great care and attention with Maude's house.

This would help her. Whatever she wanted to do.

If she wanted to stay in her home, it would be so lovely and nice for her. If she wanted to move somewhere she could be looked after, well, she wouldn't have to worry about leaving behind a messy house.

And while we worked, we laughed and chatted, and nobody had a bad thing to say about anything.

I suppose this was our end-of-year project. Our school play. Our school trip. Working together in the bright sunshine, doing something lovely. It was really nice to be a part of this team.

'CHILDREN!' exclaimed Maude when she got home to find us all sitting on the low wall around her house, all sweaty and tired. 'What have you done? The house looks perfect! It's just like it used to be!'

And as Fiona and Barry went inside to help fetch everybody a big glass of squash and a slice

of Maude's cherry cake, Dad rubbed my back. He didn't have to say anything. It was nice just feeling how happy he was. And, I think, proud.

'I thought my door was brown!' she says, tickling Baxter's tummy as he dozed on her lap. 'Turns out it's yellow. You brought out the sunshine in my house, Miss Joss!'

But the real success was how great everyone felt again. The Griffin Games gang was a team again. Nothing could go wrong now!

And then it went a bit wrong.

CHAPTER TWENTY-FOUR

When we got back to the office, the first thing we saw was the police car.

A police officer was nodding his head and taking lots of notes as Mr Jackson paced around with furious footsteps. The police car had its blue lights flickering and everything felt a bit scary.

Mr Jackson was frothing with rage and wiping his mouth.

'That's her!' he yelled, spotting me, with angry spit going everywhere. 'THAT'S the kidnapper!'

KIDNAPPER?

The police officer looked confused. He could see I was clearly a child.

'She kidnapped me! Joss Pilfrey! Tricked me and locked me in the basement!' he yells. 'And then when I managed to call YOU and get out, she'd kidnapped the WHOLE OFFICE!'

He was going wild. I noticed he was really dirty and covered in ink. His tie was halfway down to his knees. His hair was all over the place.

'Officer,' I say calmly. 'This man is obviously in some distress.'

'DISTRESS?!' shrieks Mr Jackson, waving his arms round like he's trying to swat a million flies. 'Oh, I'm DISTRESSED all right! Officer, arrest this child for kidnap, office kidnap, bad office management and illegally working as a child! And then arrest her father for allowing it to happen!'

Dad looks shocked, but I can deal with unruly people.

'Are you saying,' I say, calmly, 'that you were *kid*napped by a . . . *kid*?'

The officer frowns.

'YES!' says Mr Jackson. 'A kid who thinks she knows best about everything! Who thinks she can boss me about! Even though I AM TECHNICALLY IN CHARGE!'

'Wait,' I say. 'You were technically in charge

of a workplace . . . that let a *kid* take over?'

'YES!' says Mr Jackson.

'Then, officer,' I say, 'if what he says is true –
arrest this man!'

I just wanted to frighten Mr Jackson.

I asked the police officer not to actually arrest
him. He had been humiliated enough, I reckon.
Hopefully he learned some valuable lessons
about how to behave in public. He really has to
remember that even when he's in the car park,
he's still an ambassador for Griffin Games.

And all I'd wanted to do was get the team
back together and happy before handing
everything back to Pop Griffin. I know that's
not what Dad's plan was. But if you're going to
a job, do it well.

Anyway, even though we knew he was due
back today, we were still really surprised when
we walked in.

Waiting for us in the centre of the office, standing with his hands in his pockets and his eyebrows raised, is Pop Griffin.

He stares at us.

We're all covered in grass or flecked with paint. We're sweaty. Mr Jackson looks absolutely mad, with his hair everywhere and ink on his face.

And also, there's a *police officer*.

'Well, well, well, you're back, are you?' he asks. 'Long lunch, was it, a long lunch?'

No one knows what to say, so, 'Team-building exercise,' I try.

'I can see from the fact you have brought a police officer with you it obviously went well,' he says. 'Who are you again?'

'I'm Joss,' I say. 'From Twin Pines Primary. You put me in charge when you left, remember?'

He stares at me, reminding himself of his mad decision.

'I put . . . *you* . . . in charge?' he says. 'You're saying I put you in charge . . .'

'I don't think you realized it was Take Your Kid to Work Day,' I explain. 'And I was very smartly dressed, and I was the only person to volunteer, so . . .'

'Well, I obviously made a mistake,' Pop Griffin says, taking out a pair of half-moon glasses and sliding them up his nose. 'Because I'm looking at the results. Obviously, a mistake.'

Everyone suddenly feels very awkward as he traces a finger down a sheet full of numbers.

'Mr Griffin, she's ruined everything!' says Mr Jackson, using a spotty handkerchief to try and wipe the ink off his face. 'She treated this place like school. Made us wear uniforms. Play with toys. Paint things. Take breaks. Be nice to each other. It's sickening!'

'Did she?' says Pop.

'Yes!' says Mr Jackson. 'But I saved it. I got rid of all the toys. I got rid of the uniforms. Stopped the breaks. Took over and ruled with an iron fist!'

'And when was this?' says Pop.

'Just before you got back,' says Mr Jackson. 'Yesterday!'

Pop peers over his glasses at Mr Jackson.

'Well, yesterday is the day I'm looking at. Yesterday we did the worst we've done in years,' he says. 'Because up until then we were doing better than *ever*. Our results just kept getting better and better . . . you only had one bad day – just one bad day the whole time I was gone – and it was the day you, Mr Jackson, were in charge, Mr Jackson. Can you explain that?'

Dad nudges me. I look up at him. He winks and smiles. Then he reaches into his pocket and secretly hands me my BOSS pass.

I get it now. Dad didn't want to show what Griffin Games was like with Mr Jackson in charge – he wanted to show what it was like *without me*!

He wanted to show it wasn't a fluke, or potluck, or chance, or Mr Jackson silently steering in the background.

He didn't want to show what a bad boss Mr Jackson was. He wanted to prove what a great boss *I* am!

Do you know what? I think my dad might actually be a genius after all.

'So, Joss,' says Pop Griffin, looking at me. 'This was your doing?'

'Well, me and Dad,' I say. 'My Number One Assistant.'

CHAPTER TWENTY-FIVE

Pop wanted to know everything we'd done.

And so, twenty minutes later, the ball pit is back. And the slide. And Tim and Kareem are in their karate gear. And everyone is sitting under HIGHLY colourful and motivational posters. They've all just come in from break, and now they're on the phones, talking to their customers VERY excitedly.

'I love this new online catalogue, Tim – love it!' says Pop, and Tim is beaming. 'It's exactly right!'

Only Mr Jackson seems unhappy. He's wide-eyed with his tie still wonky, just spinning and spinning round in his chair.

'This is wonderful!' says Pop Griffin. 'Look at them all! So engaged! So excited! So engaged! I feel like buying a bunch of Griffin Games myself!'

'Um, excuse me, Mr Griffin?' says a voice. It's Angela. Pop looks surprised.

'Angela,' he says. 'Yes?'

'Um, I just wanted to hand this in?' she says, shyly. 'It's a special project that Joss asked me to do.'

Pop nods, takes the file and opens it.

'New ideas for Griffin Games!' he says, delighted. 'A Mega Office Ball Pit! An Efficiency

Sand Timer! Balls to pass round to start interesting conversations! New ideas for Griffin Games! These are games for grown-ups, Angela! A whole new market! You've been here ten years and never done anything like this! Games for Grown-ups! Genius!'

Angela looks embarrassed but proud.

'Joss asked me for my ideas,' she says. 'She trusted me with a project.'

Pop turns to me.

'Joss, you've saved Griffin Games, you have,' he says. 'Can I ask you to stay on and work here forever and ever?'

'Not really,' I say. 'I'm ten.'

He looks disappointed.

'But I'd love a summer job,' I say. 'Maybe I could be some kind of . . . Office Monitor?'

'Perfect!' says Pop. 'Okay, Office Monitor it is, okay. Now we need to organize your leaving do!'

217

It seems that one thing that really isn't any different between the grown-up world and the kid world is a love of cake. Even Sleepy Ken woke up, somehow sensing the sugar in the air. And in an office full of adults, it seems that any excuse is good enough for a cake.

Birthday? Cake.

Retirement? Cake.

Good day? Cake.

Bad day? Cake.

Wednesday? Cake.

Day a ten-year-old girl is made Office Monitor and leaves the company to go back to school? Loads of cake.

Pop Griffin sent Mr Jackson out to get them all. He promised he'd pay him back from petty cash, but I didn't see him do that. Never mind, these things happen.

At school, sometimes we're allowed to bring in toys from home on our last day of the year. At Griffin Games, we've already got a basement full of them.

Ooh, and you also get presents!

Everybody clubbed together and Angela nipped out and bought me my very own office mug.

It read: WORLD'S BEST BOSS.

'It's perfect,' I say. 'I will put it in the mug cupboard for when I'm back. And if you want to borrow it that's fine, just wash it out afterwards, please!'

Then I remembered it was my turn to do something.

I had to name my STAR OF THE WEEK!

'Look, you're all stars,' I say, standing on my chair. 'But I did want to point out one person in particular. When we were doing Project Maude, I saw that one of you was really quietly trying extra hard. Someone who once told me he usually just stays in the background and keeps out of trouble. And that was Barry.'

Everybody starts applauding Barry, who goes bright red. He wasn't expecting it to be him and he has a large slice of cake stuck halfway in his mouth. But he looks delighted and starts applauding himself and high-fiving people as he chews.

And then Angela steps forward.

'We did another special project, boss,' she says. 'Joss, this is for you.'

And she hands me a book.

'It's your end-of-job Report Card,' she says. 'We all wrote one.'

Oh, wow. Report Cards? Best. Day. Ever!

REPORT CARD ☺

Discipline A+ (but in a good way)
Creativity A++

Joss made us feel good about ourselves and listened to us.

We would work for her any time.
Signed Barry & Fiona

REPORT CARD

ENCOURAGEMENT A++
KARATE CHOPS A+

Joss always had time for us and never made us feel silly or in trouble.
Signed TIM ☺ & Kareem

REPORT C...

oh hi, I'm not really sure 😐 what's going ? on.
Signed Sleepy Ken
zzz ☺

222

And finally . . .

REPORT CARD

For being a good human A++
For being a great daughter A+++

I always tell you to grab every opportunity. You did.

But please just remember you're not in charge at home.

LOVE, Dad

And for now, that was how my last day at Griffin Games ended.

As part of a strange new family of very good friends. And Mr Jackson.

CHAPTER TWENTY-SIX

So that was how, for a little while at least, I became my own dad's boss.

When we got home, Dad made hot chocolate. He told me what he does to make it extra special, just the way I like it. He adds salted caramel. I never knew! My dad has a lot of hidden ideas that make him very special. I have to say, he really is the best dad I have ever had.

When Mum gets home, she has so many questions for us. She's reading my report cards and saying, 'But how did you do this?' and 'Bob, how did she do this?' and 'Joss, what did you say to encourage this person?', and I'm like, 'Mum, chill out with the questions! You'll find your own way!'

In the days that followed, a lot changed.

Pop Griffin decided that he had a special mission for Mr Jackson. He'd pay him a little extra money and put him completely in charge . . . *of the stockroom.* Pop said there were many, many pieces of paper that needed to be put in the right order. It was vital for the future of Griffin Games that this was done!

Mr Jackson tried to make Fiona go with him, but Fiona has really grown in confidence.

'Absolutely not, Mr Jackson,' she said, before using his mug right in front of him!

And Dad? Well, he got Mr Jackson's job. He kept the ball pit and the posters. He gave everyone lots of breaks. He let Angela start her new Games for Grown-ups catalogue and made her his deputy. He decided to keep his old desk and turn Mr Jackson's private office into an art studio for creative thinking – anyone can use it now. And he still comes to me for advice and inspiration, which I am happy to give, completely free of charge.

As for everyone else, well, we make sure we always visit Maude every day in her new home. I organized a very effective rota system and we go in pairs. Maude is delighted. She and all the other residents at Silver Birch Care Home just love seeing the 'children'. Somehow, she still thinks everyone except me is ten. Plus, we take Baxter with us, of course. Just like Maude said, she wasn't allowed to take him with her to her new home, so we adopted him as the Office Dog. Maude comes and walks him whenever she likes and each of us gets a turn to look after him, just like the school guinea pig. But if I'm honest, he spends a lot more time with Angela than anyone else. He loves sitting by her feet, in a little basket she brought in from home. She can't stop smiling these days. I know I said school pets weren't for fun, they were to teach responsibility – but now I think they can be both.

And as for me? Well, back at school, everybody wanted to hear about what I'd been up to. I even got the responsibility of leading a whole assembly! Not even Class Monitors get that honour!

I told everybody what I had learned. How what we learn at school can be really useful for the grown-up world, and about what you can achieve when you really work together and join in. Everybody clapped for ages after. Even Jack Davis looked pretty impressed. And I saw Sarah give me a shy thumbs up, which made me feel better than anything.

I go to my new school after the summer holidays. Mum seems resigned about it, but she says that she is going to miss seeing me at lunchtimes. But I've told her that I will save all my many questions about schooling for when I get home each night. I'll have lots of new things I'll want to ask her. Millions and millions of questions. For hours and hours and hours. All evening, every evening. Mum went quite pale after that. How will she spend her lunchtimes now? Chatting with colleagues? Awful.

I will be leaving Twin Pines Primary a better place than it was when I arrived. Because Pop Griffin gave my school playground a free giant

THE JOSS PILFREY HELTER-SKELTER FOR CHILDREN

helter-skelter all of its own: 'The Joss Pilfrey Helter-Skelter for Children'. I'm allowed to use it at the weekends as well as school days, if I'm not playing Swingball with Dad or hanging out with Sarah, that is.

And the other thing is I now do karate club every week. I take it very seriously. I already have a green belt and have learned moves not even the teachers know, and pretty soon I'm sure they'll let me teach there. I make sure I ask my karate teacher at least fifty questions every session. Really, really detailed questions. Ones I already sort of know the answers to, so I can always correct her if she's wrong.

I have to be quick, because I recently heard a rumour that she is trying to find somewhere else to teach. So weird.

Also, I now have karate friends there. Some of them actually go to Twin Pines too! Including Sarah, who now wears a karate outfit instead of her big blue duffle coat. I invited her to come to karate because maybe it will help with her confidence. I make sure she knows when she's doing really well. And she reminds me of all the karate facts we've memorized together. Now we do karate together every single Wednesday night and then go for cheeseburgers after.

She's going to the same new school as me.

We've promised we're going to look after each other at Woodhall Secondary. We're going to join in with stuff there. It's made me feel so much better about the change.

Sarah is my best friend.

It's really good to have one.

The End

Acknowledgements

Joss has a few more people to thank for letting her have her adventure. They all work in a completely different office, though.

She'd like to thank Rachel Denwood, who makes sure everybody takes it in turns to make the tea. Ali Dougal, who puts all the terrifying OBEY! and SHUSH! signs all over the office. Katie Lawrence, who can often be found in the stationery cupboard, because she has a terrible sense of direction and thinks it's the lobby. Lizzie Clifford, who organises all the birthday cards and makes sure all the names are spelled correctly. Eve Wersocki Morris, who flicks everyone's ears when she walks past their desk. Daniel Fricker, who secretly steals other people's sandwiches from the fridge and everyone knows it. Laura Hough, who always brings a cake in to celebrate, even if it's just your cat's birthday. Robert Kirby, who says he's working from home but has actually taken his computer to the Canary Islands. Sophie, Sean and Dani, who are actually identical triplets who stand on each others' shoulders in a long coat and pretend to be grown-ups working in an office. And Gemma Correll, who drew all the brilliant pictures in Joss's story. Oh – and thank YOU for reading!

DANNY WALLACE is an award-winning writer and radio presenter who's done lots of silly things. He's been a character in a video game, made a TV show about monkeys, and even started his own country. He has written lots of bestselling books including *Hamish and the Worldstoppers*, *The Day the Screens Went Blank* and *The Luckiest Kid in the World*.

GEMMA CORRELL is a writer, illustrator and cartoonist. In the past decade, she's collaborated with various companies to design over 400 products, co-host multiple events, and launch a magazine. Be sure to check out Gemma Correll on Instagram and her website gemmacorrell.com